Cinders & Sparrows

Cinders & Sparrows

STEFAN BACHMANN

Greenwillow Books
An Imprint of HarperCollins*Publishers*

Cinders & Sparrows

Copyright © 2020 by Stefan Bachmann

The text of this book is set in 13-point Dante MT.
Book design by Paul Zakris

Library of Congress Control Number: 2020943183
ISBN 978-0-06-228995-7 (hardback)
20 21 22 23 24 PC/LSCH 10 9 8 7 6 5 4 3 2 1
First Edition

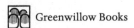 Greenwillow Books

For Hanni and Leo

Chapter One

IT was the first day of autumn when I came to Blackbird Castle, the trees copper and green, pumpkins growing along the ditch by the side of the road, a moon like a lidded silver eye already visible in the evening sky—in short, an excellent day for a witch to return to her ancestral home. But of course I knew nothing of witches then. My mind was on simpler things: the spring that had wormed its way through the velvet of the coach bench and was poking me in the back; the fact that I was cold and stiff; and also the fact that we had just stopped with a jolt in the middle of the road.

The coachman thrust his red-cheeked face through the window. "That's that, miss," he growled. "That's all the farther I'll take you."

I blinked at him. Then I clambered out of the coach, dragging my carpetbag with me. We were on a desolate mountainside, forests to my left, a precipice to my right, a river rumbling somewhere far below.

"Blackbird Castle," I asked. "Where is it?"

"Not far," the coachman said, pointing up the mountain. "If you can fly."

My gaze followed his wizened finger, my heart sinking. There was a path, stitched with bridges, wending to and fro among the cliffs and forested slopes. And far, far back, its towers barely poking over the crowns of the great old trees, were the spires of a house. A few glowing lights pierced the gloom like watchful eyes.

"I don't suppose there's any way to get the carriage up there?" I asked as politely as I could. "I paid for the full journey."

"You didn't pay me near enough to take you right

up to the Blackbirds' front door," the coachman said, and spat onto the road. His great inky horses were pawing and snorting, their breath steaming in the chilly air. "Not for all the gold in Westval . . . What's a girl like you doing going up there anyway?" His gaze darkened. "You're not one of them, are you?"

"No," I said, but what I meant was "I hope to be, very soon."

The coachman peered at me more closely, his eyes glinting like a pair of coins under the wide brim of his hat. "I trust you know the rumors? About their old witch queen, how she ate the hearts of her enemies for dinner, boiled on a bed of greens? How they've all got pairs of silver scissors hanging from their belts, and no one knows what for? And listen to this . . . Betsy Gilford once told me she crept up to a window and saw them dancing around a circle of chalk on the drawing-room floor, and all the spiders in the room were dancing with them!"

I squinted suspiciously at the coachman. "That sounds highly unlikely."

He snorted, but he looked confused. I suppose he had expected me to be frightened.

"All I'm telling you," he said, "is you'd better watch yourself. Odd things happen in these hills. Betsy Gilford's cow once wandered up that very path and was next found atop Pot's Peak, its hide written all over with gibberish."

"I think perhaps you shouldn't believe everything Betsy Gilford tells you," I said, pulling down my hat. "But thank you for the warning. I'm sure I'll be all right." I smiled at him. "They're expecting me."

The coachman guffawed. "No doubt they are." He gave me one last sharp look, which I did not like at all. Then, with a flick of his reins, he turned the coach on a precarious corner and thundered back down the mountain into the gathering gloom.

I had been the last passenger on the stagecoach. I'd boarded it in the city of Manzemir, squeezing myself in between the door and a many-chinned old lady eating plums. She had been very nice and had shared her plums with me, as well as everything I could possibly want to know about her seven children and thirty-two grand-children. But she'd disembarked at Gorlitz, and slowly, one by one, all the other passengers had gotten out too, at villages and hamlets and farms. I'd watched them embracing old acquaintances, vanishing into houses and through creaking garden gates.

It made me excited for my own journey's end. I was an orphan, and until three days ago had believed I would remain so for the rest of my life. But fate had other plans, and let me know of them in the oddest way imaginable.

I was in Mrs. Boliver's back garden, balancing on a chair, on top of another chair, on top of an enormous pink hat-box, trying to lift a cat from its precarious position atop the boiler, when the scarecrow arrived with the letter.

"Just a moment!" I called above the shrilling doorbell. The cat hissed and batted at me with its claws. It was an odd-looking thing, rather shadowy, its teeth a bit too long. In a stern voice I said to it, "Look, you're going to be stuck up there forever if you don't let me help you."

The cat gave me a supercilious stare.

"Isn't it a bit hot up there? Aren't you burning?"

Now the cat looked as if it were grinning at me. The bell rang again.

"I said *just a moment!*" I shouted, and from inside Mrs. Boliver shouted too, her ancient voice only slightly less shrill than the bell, "Who is making that infernal racket? Go answer the door, girl!"

I was employed as a maid by Mrs. Boliver, who was a widow and lived in Cricktown, far out in the middle of nowhere. Mrs. Boliver was ninety-seven and walked with a cane. As for me, I was twelve, tall and underfed, with wild black hair, the sort of hair you might call curly if you were charitable, or, if you were Mrs. Boliver, "a hopeless briar patch so bewitched by the fairies that combs and hairpins become irretrievably lost in it."

"What an extraordinary-looking girl," she had said when I'd first arrived from the orphanage, and I don't think she'd meant it as a compliment.

I must have taken too long to answer the bell,

because in the end the scarecrow clambered right over the garden wall to reach me. I had just landed with a squelch in the grass when I was confronted with a pair of legs clad in ragged paisley trousers. My gaze traveled upward until I was looking into eyes made from large silver buttons. *Oh!* I thought, flinching a little.

The scarecrow was very old, practically falling to pieces. Mushrooms grew from its face, and its coattails were rotting and mossy. But the envelope it held was not old. It was thick papered and creamy, stamped with a knobble of black wax in the shape of a raven. The scarecrow said nothing to me. It only bowed very low, handed me the letter, and then clambered back over the wall, its wooden bones creaking. I saw the top of its stovepipe hat skimming away as it sauntered down the alley.

I stood for a moment, looking at the letter. *For Zita Brydgeborn*, it said in large, coiling script, and that made me flinch all over again, for I'd not seen that name, nor heard it spoken, in ten long years.

"Who was that?" Mrs. Boliver asked, hobbling up next to me.

"A scarecrow," I said, and Mrs. Boliver nodded grimly. She did not hear very well, but she didn't like to admit it.

"And what have you got there?"

"A letter."

"For me?"

"No," I said, not quite believing it myself. "I think . . . I think it's for me!"

Mrs. Boliver squinted at the envelope through her little spectacles. "Zita *who?*" she demanded, giving me a resentful once-over, as if seeing me for the first time as a human girl and not a walking broom. And then I could not wait a second longer. I ran up to my attic, my heart squirming in my chest, and for a good minute I simply sat on the floor, cradling the letter in my hands. It was like a beacon, this letter, or a life ring tossed into a stormy sea. I was no longer adrift in the world. Someone, somewhere, knew I existed. Fingers trembling, I broke the seal.

Dear Miss Zita Brydgeborn, the letter began, and again

my heart gave a strange little lurch. That name was secret. Everyone knew me as Ingabeth, because that was the name the great wimpled nun had given me upon my arrival at the orphanage. I'd been two, and according to orphanage lore, had been left on the doorstep precisely at sunset, my hair full of twigs and the rest of me entirely covered in soot.

"Think you're the queen of everything, do you?" the nun had said, while I'd sat on a chair in the front hall. "Zita, indeed . . . what a frivolous name for a little girl no one wanted!"

And so I'd tucked the name away, a little treasure all for myself. No one else should have known it. And yet someone did.

Dear Miss Zita Brydgeborn,

I write to you as the solicitor of the Brydgeborn estate. I have reason to believe you are the sole heir to Blackbird Castle and its environs, as well as any monies, accounts, lands, and property within. I bid you come at your earliest convenience to

*Blackbird Castle, north of Hackenden village, in the Westval,
where, if it can be proven you are the heir, we will complete the
paperwork posthaste.*

Your humble servant,

Charles Grenouille, Dubney & Sons, Esquire

Of course, I hadn't believed the letter right away. I'd
walked to the post office and asked about the address.
"From the Brydgeborns of Westval," the clerk had said,
looking down at me incredulously from behind his desk.
"Very great family. Very important. Whyever would the
Brydgeborns send a letter to *you*?"

I'd told him I had no idea. I still had no idea. But I was
not about to let such an invitation go unanswered, and
so twelve hours later I left Mrs. Boliver and set off on
the steam train to Hackenden, my wages inside my coat
pocket and a new hat on my head.

It had been a much longer journey than I had expected.
Steam train turned to donkey cart, which turned back to
steam train, until at last, three days later, I'd boarded the

post coach in Manzemir. I had been ready to burst from my skin the entire way, the excitement dulling every jolt and rattle. It was a lovely thing, feeling that perhaps I had my own door and welcoming embraces waiting, that perhaps I was going home.

Chapter Two

THE woods reared up above me, wild and twisting, a dark mass of evergreens and gnarled oaks. Night was falling quickly, and I could hear the infinite layers of sound from the forest's depths, the hoot of owls, the whispering of leaves, the creak of branches . . . the rustle of small paws in the undergrowth, and then a sudden cry as the creature was caught.

Well, better get on with it, I thought, hoisting my bag onto my shoulder. And shrugging off my weariness, I began to climb.

It was a steep, tiresome journey. The steps were made

of coiled roots. Rocks jutted overhead and shrubs pressed close on either side, but the path wasn't quite overgrown. At least that meant someone lived up there. I had begun to wonder if perhaps this was all an elaborate scheme to get a foolish servant girl into the middle of nowhere to rob her. Then again, the joke would be on the robbers, going through all this trouble for the contents of my carpetbag. It contained everything I owned in the world, which was hardly anything—a toothbrush, a bar of soap, a wooden comb I had been given upon leaving the orphanage. My friends had put together their pennies and bought it for me the day I left, scratching their names into the bone handle with a pin. Other than that, there was only a threadbare nightgown and a Sunday bonnet with a large purple flower on it. If the robbers fancied the bonnet, I'd let them know they could have it.

The sun was completely gone by the time I reached the top. The moon, red and rusting, seemed to watch me from between the snow-covered peaks. I passed under an eerie Gothic archway, all twisted vines and goblin faces, and trudged up some steps.

I could make out the house more clearly now. It was not exactly a castle, though it had towers and battlements, and not precisely a palace or a mansion either. It might have been all of those things at one point, but parts of it looked abandoned, and parts looked as if they had burned down, and so there were grand bits, and fancy bits, and ancient, pagan, strange bits, all sewn up with copious amounts of black ivy. Only one or two windows were lit, very high up, and curtains were drawn against the panes, giving the light a red, warning hue.

I climbed the steps, past several terraces of overgrown shrubbery and a fountain, now quite dry. At the front doors, I set down my carpetbag with a gasp. I smoothed my coat, arranged my hat, took a deep breath, took another deep breath for good measure. . . . Then I gripped the great brass knocker, which had been wrought to look like the nose ring of a scowling three-toothed ogre. "Sorry, old chap," I said, letting the knocker fall against the ogre's chin.

The sound it made was not at all what I had expected. It was like a bell, far off and mournful. It tolled once, and even the woods seemed to go still, as if they too anticipated whatever lay behind these doors.

Would a butler answer? Or a footman? Or a shrunken housekeeper with a single candle illuminating the grooves in her face? I had been the only servant at Mrs. Boliver's and was hardly an expert in grand houses. But I didn't expect *nothing*, and nothing was exactly what happened.

I waited. I walked around a corner to peek in a darkened window. I stood back, hands on my hips, to survey the towers and roofs. . . .

Behind me in the woods, I heard the trees creaking, boughs whispering in their cunning language. When I spun to face them, I could have sworn there were eyes among the branches, dark and cold, watching me.

Just when I was sure I had made a terrible mistake and I'd better run back down the mountain, carpetbag flailing, and beg Mrs. Boliver to hire me again, I heard the sound of many locks being unlocked and bolts being drawn back, and a much smaller door swung open in a corner of the great doors. A lit candelabra floated in the dark beyond, clutched in a plump, pale hand.

"Oh!" said a voice, presumably belonging to the hand. "Oh, it's you! Come in, come in, quick!"

I ducked in gratefully, and as my eyes adjusted to the darkness, I saw the candelabra was held by a maid. *Like me!* I thought, feeling instantly more at ease. I smiled at her, and she smiled back and curtsied. I'd never been curtsied to before. I curtsied too, not wanting to be rude. This only made her giggle, until another figure emerged from the shadows and poked her shoulder. This person was a very tall boy in a black uniform; it looked like a cross between a soldier's and a footman's.

"Minnifer!" he scolded under his breath. "Are you seven?"

"It's all right," I said, glancing between them. The boy was melancholy looking, his brows dark. Minnifer was short and round, and she had little twinkling eyes and a neat bun of brown hair.

"We're so glad you came," said Minnifer. "We hope you'll love it here."

"We do," said the boy, in a very soft, very polite voice.

"I'm Minnifer," said Minnifer. "And he's Bram."

She curtsied again, and Bram bowed, and they reminded me suddenly of wooden dolls on strings, standing there in their neat black clothes.

"I'm very pleased to meet both of you," I said, shaking their hands. "I'm Zita."

Bram and Minnifer continued to smile awkwardly, as if they weren't quite sure what to do with me.

"She might like to eat," Bram murmured to Minnifer. "We have all those leftovers from dinner."

"Or she might like a bath," said Minnifer, sizing me up. "Did you walk the whole way from Hackenden?"

"You'd think so, wouldn't you?" I said, adjusting my hat for what felt like the twentieth time that evening. "But no, just up the hill."

"Minnifer," said Bram, shaking his head. "You practically called her filthy."

"I did not! I offered her a bath! That's *manners*."

"She just doesn't think very often," said Bram to me.

"And Bram thinks so much he forgets to breathe sometimes," said Minnifer. "In fact, you'll find us all insufferable once you get to know us. Now, how about food *and* a bath, and then—"

Just as I was thoroughly charmed by both of them, another voice sounded from the top of the stairs. A ball of light from a kerosene lamp was descending toward us, and I saw for the first time the enormous hall that we were standing in. The floor was a checkerboard of black-and-white marble. A chandelier in the shape of a flock of crows attacking a serpent hung from the ceiling. Tapestries lined the walls, their faded threads depicting parties of men and women in black cloaks and pointy shoes trooping through woods and fording rivers. And on the landing of the staircase, half illuminated by the lamp in her hand, stood a woman.

She was very pretty, very pale. Her fingers were encrusted with jewels, like some sort of sprouting multi-colored fungus. Her auburn hair was swept up into lacquered curls, and her dress was deep blue silk, dark and frothy as the breakers against a nighttime shore. I could not tell if she was young or old—she looked confusingly ageless—and as she stood there on the landing, one arm curled around the newel post, I felt she reminded me most of a glamorous cat.

"There'll be no baths," she said, in the loveliest, chilliest breath of a voice I had ever heard. "And she can have a tray in her room. No need to make a fuss. Mr. Grenouille will be here in the morning to sort out this . . . unfortunate mistake."

Mistake? My heart sank. I could tell by the way she looked at me that the "unfortunate mistake" was me, standing there in my scuffed shoes and patched coat.

"Good evening, ma'am," I said, forcing my chin up. "I don't mean to be a bother, and I'm sorry to arrive so late, but—"

"Late?" said the lady, gliding down the stairs and across the tiles toward me. "But are you? Zita was lost *all* these years, and now a girl claiming to be her comes waltzing back as soon as there's a castle to inherit? Rather *too* punctual, I should say."

She leaned down, so close I could smell the rose-tinted powder on her cheeks. "I'll be perfectly honest with you: either Mr. Grenouille is a fool, or you are a liar." She lifted my chin with two long, elegant fingers. "You're not a Blackbird, are you? You've got the look of a housemaid!"

"I *am* a housemaid," I said, twitching away from her grasp. "But I got a letter, and my name's Zita, just like it says." I pulled the letter out of my pocket and held it up for her to see.

The lady's eyes flickered to the black wax seal. "A letter was sent, yes. Whether the real Zita Brydgeborn ever received it is another matter. Of course you were aware this family is the most powerful—and indeed *last*—of the reigning witch families of old?"

"W-witch families?" This time I could not keep the

stammer out of my voice. Had the coachman not been fibbing at all? "There was nothing about that in the—"

"And you've never read a history book?" she inquired pleasantly, relishing my discomfort.

"Not one with witches in it," I whispered.

The lady drew back, her blue eyes shifting slightly. Then she pursed her lips in some secret amusement and said, "How convenient. Well, whether you are a Brydgeborn or not will be made *quite* clear in the morning. You two . . . find someplace to put her." And with that, she swept away, vanishing into the murk of the hall.

I gaped after her. Bram tried to take my carpetbag, but I shook him off. I wasn't wanted here, that much was clear. I wasn't going to give these people any reason to make me beholden to them.

"Who was *she*?" I demanded.

"A wicked goat," said Bram.

"And terribly rich," Minnifer added in an awestruck whisper. "Ysabeau Harkleath-St. Cloud. A Cantanker by marriage, and a great friend of your mother's. The custodians gave her temporary responsibility of the house after . . . well, after everything that happened."

My mother. The word sent the faintest fluttering memory of violets and rosemary straight to my heart.

"What do you mean, 'everything that happened'?" I asked as Minnifer opened a panel in the wall, and she and Bram led me up a wrought-iron servants' staircase. "What did happen? Where is everyone?"

Again Minnifer and Bram exchanged that odd, inscrutable look. "Gone," said Minnifer softly. And then she turned to me suddenly, the candlelight throwing a ruddy shadow across her face. "You've got to be careful, Zita. They're all dead. All of the Brydgeborns. Your mother and father, aunts and uncles. No one's left. No one but you."

"Oh!" I said, half delighted to be made aware of such an extensive family, half horrified to be informed they were dead.

"Murdered—" Minnifer started to say, before her mouth clamped shut like a bear trap. Her eyes bulged.

She struggled for a moment, her fingers clawing at her jaw. Then her mouth popped open again and she turned away, hunched over the stairs and crying.

"What on *earth?*" I murmured. "What was that? Are you all right?"

I turned to Bram, but he was only watching helplessly, his hands clenched at his sides.

"I'm fine," Minnifer snuffled, probing at her cheeks with one cautious finger. "It was just a hiccup."

That wasn't like any hiccup I've ever heard, I thought, but Minnifer was already climbing the stairs again, so quickly Bram and I had to run to catch up.

We exited the servants' staircase and crossed a landing, past two small windows. The windows were side by side, only inches apart, but one of them looked into an ivy-shrouded court in the dead of night, and the other onto a misty field at twilight, its rows full of frosted pumpkins and a few solitary scarecrows. I barely had time to wonder about it, however, before we were climbing another staircase, and a third. At last we arrived in a high corridor, in front of a lovely gilded door painted with windmills and sky.

"Here we are," said Bram, his voice now very low and angry.

"Mrs. Cantanker didn't say which room to give you," said Minnifer, wiping her nose on the back of her hand. "And there are thirty-seven bedrooms to choose from. But we thought you'd like this one best."

"Don't go any farther down this passage," said Bram, unlocking the door. "It has been known to lead to places one might rather not visit."

"Don't go into the room labeled Parlor of Psychosis," said Minnifer. "And if you see a blue staircase, do *not* climb it."

"You know, it might be best if you didn't leave your room," said Bram quickly. "We'll come for you in the morning."

They led me into a dark chamber with three big windows overlooking the desolate gardens I had passed on my arrival.

"Is this all for me?" I asked, turning a circle. I'd never had a room to myself, especially not one so grand, and even at Mrs. Boliver's I'd shared my attic with a family of cockroaches and one enormous rat.

"Of course it's all for you," said Bram distractedly, and Minnifer mumbled, "What *is* she talking about?"

Bram lit a second candelabra. Minnifer promised to bring up a kettle of hot water for washing. Then, with anxious looks, they left the room, closing the door behind them. I heard them whispering outside. A moment later the key turned twice, softly, and they were gone.

Chapter Three

I woke the next morning to find a crow sitting on my chest, peering down at me with the disconcerting gaze of something that might like to take a great juicy bite out of one of my eyeballs. Its own eyes were bright black droplets nestled among the blue sheen of its feathers. I could feel its weight, heavy on the sheets, claws pricking the comforter. The room was freezing, the air slightly damp, as if I were out of doors.

The crow and I stared at each other for a long moment. Then I screeched at the top of my lungs, kicking at the sheets. The bird let out an indignant caw and flapped over to the mantelpiece, where it looked over its feathered shoulder at me as if in reproach. A second later, it flew into the chimney and began wriggling its way up it, sending showers of soot onto the hearth.

Immediately, I forgot my fear and leaped out of bed. I ran to the chimney and peered up it, waving away the soot. "Don't do that!" I called out. "You'll get stuck!"

A sparrow had once gotten stuck in the chimney in Mrs. Boliver's parlor. Smoke had billowed out, staining every doily and lacy pillow black, and when I'd poked the broom handle up to find the blockage, the sparrow had fallen into the ashes, closely followed by six roasted hatchlings and a nest. The mother sparrow had gone down the chimney's flaming throat, foolish and brave, to stop whatever glowing monster had been cooking her offspring. I'd been very upset by the incident and had buried the little creatures in the back garden next to Mrs. Boliver's extensive cemetery of goldfish.

This crow seemed to know exactly what it was doing, however. The noise of its efforts became quieter and quieter, then ceased altogether. I hoped that meant the bird had popped out the top.

When the crow was gone and the chimney was silent once more, I got up from the hearth and peered around the room. I'd only seen snatches of it the night before, fleeting glimpses revealed by the light of the candelabra. Now, by day, the chamber was even grander than I had imagined. The bed was as large as a coach, a four-poster hung with periwinkle velvet. The floor was laid with sumptuous carpets. And every surface, every mirror and pane of glass, was covered in frost.

I stepped into the center of the room, eyeing the fuzz that glittered on the tapestries and furniture. *How odd,* I thought. *Frost must come early to these mountains.* Outside, the trees were just turning rich shades of russet and bronze, their leaves escaping their anchors and swirling in the air. Light flooded through the great mullioned windows, warm and golden, like apple cider. I ran forward and threw open a casement, breathing deeply of the crisp mountain air.

My room overlooked what might have once been a hedge maze, but was now all twigs and thorns, thread-bare against the lichened stone and blazing leaves. I could see the whole front of the castle, rising up around me in points and gables and little crooked windows. I could see the woods too, not nearly so frightening by day, making a ring around the gardens. It was beautiful here, in a wild, forgotten sort of way.

A knock sounded from the door. I hurried to it and tried the handle. It was unlocked. I poked my head out, and there was Bram standing in the hall, his hat in his hands. He looked as if he had just come in from outside, rosy faced and smelling of the cold.

"Are you hungry?" he asked, without any sort of preamble.

"Starving," I said. "Good morning."

"All right. You can eat with us. I'm afraid Mrs. Cantanker said you weren't to be in the formal rooms until—"

"Until they've decided I'm not a guttersnipe?"

"Well, I'm not sure she used quite those words. But we eat just as well as they do, don't worry. I'll come back to collect you once you've dressed."

He ducked his head and retreated down the corridor.

I closed the door and stared at it a moment. Then I smiled. Things were already looking up. I decided I wouldn't mind much if there *had* been a mistake, if the wrong Zita had been summoned and I was sent away again. I had made it all my life without a castle or an inheritance, and I was sure I could last all the rest of it without one too. I decided to make the most of this adventure while it lasted.

I had only my dusty traveling clothes to wear, so I approached the huge old wardrobe and opened both doors. A great puff of pine and powdered roses wafted out to greet me, and I saw before me the most splendid array of clothes I had ever laid eyes upon. There were gowns in all different colors, from ruby to turquoise to dark, shadowy green. Lovely black hats too, and a mirror for adjusting, and dozens of pairs of shoes with bright silk bows and velvet laces, fur-lined ponchos, great fluffy overcoats, splendid morning robes in flowery brocade, as well as quite a number of black capes and black gloves, and little drawers full of jewelry.

It was all much too grand for me. And yet . . . *Surely no one would mind if I borrowed just one thing.* Perhaps no one even remembered this clothing was here. And if they did, and they minded, at least I'd have gotten to wear such finery once in my life before I was thrown out on my ear.

I selected a gown the color of fog and mist rising from marshes, and I slipped it on. For a moment it felt too small, like it was made for someone short and broad. But then something extraordinary happened: the threads seemed to rearrange themselves, tickling across my skin, and to my delight I looked at myself in the mirror and saw the hem stretching downward and the sleeves scurrying to reach my wrists. A moment later the dress fit as if it had been made for me.

I let my breath out slowly, running a finger over the fabric. The dress had a great ballooning skirt and whalebone stays, and all of it clicked together on its own, jerking me suddenly upright. I squeaked a little, but then leaned into it, realizing this was less a dress and more a means of conveyance, which you could ride in like an automobile. No wonder rich people always seemed so proud. Their clothes did not allow for anything else.

I did my hair as best I could, patting it down with water and trying in vain to make it point all in one direction. Then I walked several circles around the room, feeling ever more pleased with the gown and my decision to wear it. In a fit of confidence, I lifted my chin and sailed out into the hallway, the silky skirts swishing around my ankles.

Bram was just outside, leaning against the wall and chewing a stalk of dry grass. His eyes went wide when he saw me. For a moment I was flattered because I thought I looked lovely too. But then his thundercloud-black eyebrows dropped, and he said, "Come on, miss. Quickly. I'm not sure what Mrs. Cantanker will think of that."

"Oh," I said, my courage suddenly deserting me and running away down the corridor. "I just thought—"

"The dress is very nice," said Bram. He looked pained

and began walking briskly away. I ran to catch up, wondering if this had been a bad idea after all. We went down the tiny wrought-iron stair again, into the bowels of the house, to a servants' hall with garlic and lavender drying along the vaults of the ceiling. Beyond its archways, I could just make out a hive of kitchens, pantries, and cellars. I was expecting them to be bustling with cooks and scullery maids, but there was only Minnifer, sitting atop a mountain of pillowcases and mending one with a spool of blue thread. She waved at me, her face alight. But her expression fell too when she saw the dress.

"Oh," she said. "Oh, I'm not sure that was a good idea."

"My traveling clothes are all dirty," I said weakly. "I thought—"

"No, it's all right," said Minnifer. "It's just . . . well, that was *her* dress, you see? She was going to wear it for her birthday. Only she never got the chance."

"Who?" I asked. "There's no point being mysterious about it. Whose room did you put me in?"

"Greta's," said Minnifer, looking down at the

pillowcases. "Greta Brydgeborn. The young mistress."

I shivered, and the lovely garment felt suddenly uncomfortable, the bone stays biting into my back. *All of the Brydgeborns are dead. . . .*

"I'm sorry," I said. "I don't know why I took it. I'll go put it back."

And I would have too, but when I turned, there was Mrs. Cantanker standing in the doorway, staring at me with terrible, tightly wound fury. She was clad all in purple this morning, a severe dress with the cut of a gentleman's frock coat, silver buttons running across her chest to her neck, and skirts that flared in the back like the sails of a ship.

"What is the meaning of this?" she demanded, and I remained stock-still, caught in her gaze.

"I thought no one would mind," I said quietly. "I'm . . . I'm . . ."

Sorry, I was about to say, but the word did not quite reach my lips. Instead, a sudden fury boiled up inside me and I snapped, *"Annoyed."*

Minnifer gasped. Bram looked horrified. But there was no turning back now. "No one's told me anything since I arrived here. Who are the Brydgeborns? What happened to Greta? *Am* I the heir? Or am I just expected to stumble about making a fool of myself until you throw me out? I received *one* letter and a very rude welcome, and now I'd like to know what I've been dragged into, thank you *very much.*"

I was practically shouting. Mrs. Cantanker gave me a look of disdain. But I was not going to be cowed by her now. I flashed her a glare to melt iron and noted with some satisfaction a flicker of alarm in her eyes. Then she pinched her lips together and swept forward, dragging me out of the kitchens by the arm.

"Mr. Grenouille is waiting," she snapped, her rings pressing into my skin. "This way, whoever you are, and stop shrieking. You sound like a dying rabbit."

She pulled me up the stairs and into the front hall. Then we turned through a pair of high mahogany doors, into a room that was hung with painted silk scrolls and whose windows looked out across a desolate rose garden. The lamps were not lit, but a fire was roaring and breakfast was laid. A tiny plump gentleman of about fifty was sitting at the table, hunched over a plate of eggs and steaming potato cakes.

He stood in a flurry at our arrival, looking at me as if he'd seen a ghost, which in a way I suppose he had. But he recovered almost at once, shedding his surprise with a shiver, like a little dog after a bath, and came forward, smiling nervously.

"Zita Brydgeborn! It is *good* to see you—"

"Oh, sit down, Charles," said Mrs. Cantanker. "We're not sure she's anyone yet. No doubt the gutters are crawling with girls who, with a little rouge and Tipwick's Raven Hair Dye, could be made to look like one of the Brydgeborn Blackbirds."

The lawyer cast Mrs. Cantanker a frightened look and drew me hurriedly to the table. "Will you eat with us, child? I'm sure you don't mind, Ysabeau. *Do* you mind? I hope not. I've always found one should discuss difficult subjects over delicious delicacies, as it makes them easier to digest—the difficult subjects, if not the delicacies."

Mrs. Cantanker glared at Mr. Grenouille, and I sat down quickly in front of the feast before the offer could be taken back. It was the grandest food I had ever seen. There were eggs and bacon, peaches bobbing like gleaming islands out of glossy peaks of Chantilly cream, mountains of golden potato cakes, a small bowl of hothouse raspberries, and a lovely bronze-glazed pastry that fell to buttery flakes at the touch of a fork. I wondered if I could take any of it to Minnifer and Bram. Then again, they probably ate the leftovers anyway, and who would stop them? I heaped my plate with as much food as it would hold and set to work with my fork and knife, glancing sharply at Mrs. Cantanker and Mr. Grenouille between bites.

Mrs. Cantanker looked horrified. But Mr. Grenouille watched me eagerly, one perfectly round spot of red on each cheek. I would have found him tiresome had he not had such a merry, guileless face. He wore spectacles, and his chin was receding, and so was his hairline. In fact, everything about him was receding, as if he was shrinking away from the world as far as he could without actually turning inside out or imploding.

I liked him at once. I always felt I could trust worried, anxious people more than brash ones. Those who strode through life too bravely always struck me as either foolishly unaware of the world's terrors, or else frighteningly powerful and immune to them, neither of which I found endearing. Mr. Grenouille, losing faith in his sentences, regretting every gesture, was someone I felt would not harm a fly, or a housemaid. As for Mrs. Cantanker, lounging in the periphery like a storm cloud, watching us both intently, well . . . I felt no such certainty with her.

Once I'd eaten and Mr. Grenouille had inquired after my travels and my life so far, he said, "Now. I suppose we might talk business? There is much for you to catch up on." Mrs. Cantanker raised her eyebrows and blinked down at her kippers and toast. "You say you remember nothing of your early childhood. I suppose you wouldn't. You were so tiny when. . . when you left. But you *are* aware that yours is one of the last great families of witches on the continent?"

"Mrs. Cantanker told me," I said. "I didn't really believe it. Of course I've heard about witches, and Mrs. Boliver once took a train to visit one about her gout. But they seemed awfully important and far away. I never would have thought they'd have anything to do with me." I set down my fork and squinted at the lawyer. "Mr. Grenouille, what happened to the Brydgeborns? Where are they?"

"Well . . . ," said Mr. Grenouille, plucking at his shirt cuffs and avoiding my gaze. "They're here. In the castle."

My hand twitched, rattling the silverware. *Here?* But Minnifer had said they were dead! A wild hope sprang up inside me. How lovely would it be if my welcome last night had been a strange little joke and my family was waiting for me, and I would meet them soon!

"She doesn't understand," said Mr. Grenouille to himself. "She will have to *see*." Then he turned to Mrs. Cantanker and said, "Ysabeau? Will you open up the dining room?"

Mrs. Cantanker looked at us both with an air of grave and graceful mourning, as if we had asked her to perform some terrible task. Then she rose and glided toward the door, taking a chatelaine from the folds of her gown. A great many keys in all shapes and sizes hung from the velvet tassel, tinkling quietly. "Follow me," she said.

We crossed the hall to a pair of tall gilt doors. Mrs. Cantanker unlocked them and pushed one open. Beyond was a dark cavernous space. The drapes were drawn over the windows, and only the faintest bit of morning light shone down through the leaves and detritus on a skylight high above.

"They're in here," said Mrs. Cantanker grimly, standing aside. "Please, step in. Join them."

I shuddered, peering into the room. Cobwebs had made empires of the chandeliers, linking them together with bridges and roads, gossamer threads leaping from gilded vaults to crystal branches, gray veils enshrouding the windows. I brushed one aside and trod carefully forward into the gloom. My feet sank into centimeters of dust, soft as velvet.

I heard nothing, not a breath, only the occasional sound of doves cooing and rats scuttling in the walls. I approached the table. A terrible stench brushed my nose, and between the high backs of the chairs, I saw rotting heaps of food, a tower of furred blackened fruit, a sagging cake, a leg of ham swarming with flies and glistening beetles. I covered my nose and mouth with my hand. . . . And then, with a start, I saw them: the Brydgeborns, sitting upright at their places.

They seemed to have melted, like candles, all over the chairs and the tablecloth. Drips of a waxy blue-gray film hung suspended from their fingertips, from noses and black brocade sleeves. But the substance was only a cocoon. The figures beneath it were flawlessly preserved, peering out as if from under the ice on a winter lake. A tall woman with a hooked nose sat at the head of the table. On her left and right were a bespectacled boy and a girl several years older than me.

I approached the girl's chair slowly, revulsion and curiosity overtaking me. I could see her clearly through the strange veil. She had golden hair and a heart-shaped face. Her eyes were wide open—green as pine needles—and her lips were quirked into an odd little smile, as if her death had come as no shock to her. I reached out to touch the substance that had enshrined her. It was as hard and cool as marble.

I turned, staring in horror at Mrs. Cantanker and Mr. Grenouille, who stood silhouetted in the doorway. Then I fled the room, dust and cobwebs billowing behind me as I made my escape.

"What happened to them?" I whispered, once I was back in the comparative brightness of the hall. "How did they die?"

Mrs. Cantanker closed the door, locking it firmly. "Ephinadym mulsion," she said. "A very nasty spell. Kills its victims instantly, filling every pore, every organ and vein with an indeterminate substance that cannot be broken, cracked, or melted. One minute the Brydgeborns were sitting down to an excellent dinner . . . and the next they were dead. They had no chance to defend themselves."

I stared at the closed door. "That was my mother? My mother, brother, and sister?"

"They would be your adopted brother and sister, *if* you are who you claim to be," Mrs. Cantanker said. "John and Greta Brydgeborn were not Georgina's true children."

"Zita was her first and only," said Mr. Grenouille quietly. "I'm sorry you had to meet them like this."

I swallowed, my heart aching. I had not known these people. But I should have. I should have known them my whole life, and now I never would.

"Most of the servants fled when they discovered what had happened," said Mrs. Cantanker. "They knew the implications."

"What implications?" I asked.

"The implications of such a spell having been performed in *this* house, of all houses. A house that was supposed to be a bastion against the dark arts. The implication that *something* crept in, past the woods, past the salt and iron and ancient wards, and killed one of the most powerful witches in the world, all but ending her bloodline."

"So you're saying they were murdered!" I said. "And they're just *sitting in there*? Shouldn't we call the constable—?"

"The constable?" Mrs. Cantanker tittered into her hand, a gesture I thought stupidly childish for one so elegant and refined. "And how would the constable help us? Handbills on lampposts? Ads in newspapers? 'Wanted: a pernicious murderer, well versed in the casting of intricate thousand-year-old spells'? Save your bright ideas for your diary, little girl. The enemies of the Blackbirds are not the sort the mortal world has any sway over."

I stared at her, stung by the disdain in her voice. "But who did it?" I asked. "How did the murderers get in, and what if—?" I stopped before the words spilled out. *What if they're still here?*

"Zita," said Mr. Grenouille, coming forward and taking both my hands. "I know you're from Cricktown, so your knowledge of the politics of witchery and the netherworld is patchy at best. But it's very unlikely the murderer was human. Or even alive. There are only a few things powerful enough to perform such a spell, and none of them reside in the lands of the living."

I blinked, feeling lost in that great hall, the checkerboard tiles at my feet, the painted wings of the blackbirds forming a crown above my head. Mrs. Cantanker watched me, the keys tinkling in her hands.

"You mean . . . ," I said in a small voice, "You mean the murderer was a ghost?"

"I'm afraid so," said Mr. Grenouille. And then he took out his pocket watch and consulted it ceremoniously. "But you needn't trouble yourself now! Oh no. Plenty of time to be troubled later. I'm delighted to say I've drawn up all the papers, and we'll have you installed as the new mistress of Blackbird Castle in a blink, just this way, hurry hurry!"

I felt numb to my fingertips as they led me away from that dreadful room. But even in my daze I heard them whispering to each other, Mrs. Cantanker's voice low and prickling.

"Let us not get ahead of ourselves, Charles," she murmured. "I'll not risk a false Blackbird in this house, not with the consequences so dire." She turned to me, her head cocked, and it made me think of the monstrous blue jays in Mrs. Boliver's garden, how they watched their struggling prey before pulling it to bits. "First, before anything else, we shall have to perform the test."

Chapter Four

WHAT *have I gotten myself into?* I thought as we once again traversed the great hall, Mr. Grenouille scurrying from black tile to black tile like a tiny, anxious beetle, Mrs. Cantanker flowing ahead like a stormy waterspout far out at sea, and me clumping after them in my sensible shoes and borrowed finery, feeling ever more anxious and out of place. *First witches, then murder, and now a test?*

I'd been taught to read at the orphanage. I'd devoured every line and scrap of writing in that chilly old place, and sometimes I'd even crept into the Mother Superior's office while she was snoring at her desk and stolen the books from her shelves. I knew all sixty-seven ways to prepare the most tasteless, unappetizing porridge possible, and also how to fix a wool-spinning machine if it jammed, since those had been the Mother Superior's favorite things to read about. But that was where my education ended. I didn't suppose I'd do very well at this test, whatever it was.

"Ysabeau, please," Mr. Grenouille said, breathless in his efforts to keep up. "Do you have any idea how long I searched for this girl? She *is* the Brydgeborn heir, I guarantee it—"

Mrs. Cantanker waved the lawyer's words away. "She'll have to prove that first, Charles. Don't be gullible. If she doesn't have the talent, what's the point? We might as well dress up one of the goats in petticoats and call *that* the heir of the Brydgeborns."

"What sort of talent do I need to have?" I asked, and Mrs. Cantanker gave Mr. Grenouille a pointed look as if to say, *See?*

Then she swept up the stairs, skirts rustling. "We'll go

to the Vine Room. That should be an excellent test of her ability."

"Ysabeau! Do you think that wise—"

"Aristotelian," snapped Mrs. Cantanker, her eyes fixed straight ahead.

"Ysabeau, I must protest. If she fails, she will be ripped limb from limb! Or worse!"

"What could possibly be worse than being ripped limb from limb?" I started to say, but Mrs. Cantanker interrupted.

"Excellent! Then we'll pack her up in a hatbox and send her back third-class cargo. It'll save her the cost of a full-fare ticket."

I let out an indignant gasp. Mrs. Cantanker smiled widely over her shoulder at me. "I jest, of course," she said, though I was sure she didn't. "Oh, all right. We'll go to the High Blackbird's study. But don't think you'll be able to fool me, girl. There will be no reward for trickery, and you'll find you'll rue the day you became a Blackbird for fine jewels and pretty dresses. A true Blackbird is graced with cunning, sly wits, a sharp tongue, and the power to repel the evils of night and fog. *But!* In return, they bear a great burden and are feared by both the living and the dead."

Mr. Grenouille shook his head, but he could not bring himself to protest this claim. I looked between them, becoming more confused by the second. I had traveled here to be reunited with my family, not to become a *witch*. . . .

We went up a monstrously grand staircase carved from wood so dark it appeared almost black. A reddish sheen glowed in its grain, as if blood ran deep in its veins. The entire thing was built to look like a twisting dragon, the banister scaled, the spindles fashioned into claws and folded wings. We turned up another staircase and another, each one becoming progressively narrower and less ornate. No guests came here, I supposed, no one who needed to be cowed by grand halls and dragon staircases. I felt strangely honored.

Finally, at the top of the steepest, narrowest stair of

all, we arrived at a large tower room. A beautiful stained-glass skylight dappled everything in petals of blue and green light, and every inch of the space below was filled of wonders: I spotted an aquarium filled with fish that seemed to be on fire. A golden cage in which slumbered a fuzzy, purple-winged moth the size of a small dog. A table covered with ingenious contraptions and bottles and curling glass tubes. I wandered, awestruck, past a sumptuous globe, taller than I was, with many little black crosses piercing its crust. Some were solitary, far out among the wastes and woods, but most stood in huddles around cities and towns. And when I looked up, I saw bookshelves, rising foot after foot, breathtaking cliffs of stories and secrets going all the way to the roof. Even the pillars were filled with books, little brass pegs running up them so you could reach the highest shelves.

I gasped. I'd never seen so many books in my life, not at the orphanage and certainly not at Mrs. Boliver's; she bought novels twice a year and let them molder under her coffee cups. Here there were enormous grimoires bound in oxblood- and verdigris-colored leather, books with tasseled placeholders, locked with coiling salamanders. There were rows of encyclopediae stamped with gold. There were rather dirty, unassuming volumes no larger than chapbooks that looked as if they had traveled through fire and mud. I wanted to peek inside every one of them and run my fingers over the soft pages. I wanted to sit on the floor and read every line, every ancient, exciting tale.

Mrs. Cantanker went to an enormous desk and seated herself behind it, observing me imperiously. Small pewter picture frames littered its surface, no doubt displaying members of the Brydgeborn family, but they had all been snapped facedown.

"I've got just the test," she said, lifting a large silver dish out of a drawer and setting it on the desk. Next she brought out a knife and an odd sort of fork.

"Are you a witch too?" I asked, and she smiled oddly and raised her chin, a gesture halfway between bitterness and pride.

"I have some knowledge," she said, standing and filling the silver dish with water from a mossy spigot in the wall. Then she cut several strands of rosemary and milkweed with the knife and threw them into the water, along with a few flakes of ash, swirling it all together with the fork.

"Look into the dish," Mrs. Cantanker commanded. "There is a spirit in this room. If you have talent, the scrying dish will reveal its whereabouts to you. If you have none . . ." She set down the knife and fork on a snowy linen napkin and folded it over them. "If you have none, Mr. Grenouille will return you to whichever vile alley he dredged you from. All clear?"

Mr. Grenouille mumbled something apologetic and fiddled with a button on his waistcoat. I frowned and peered into the glistening waters. I hoped I had talent. I hoped I would see *something*. But I saw only the ornate ceiling, curved like a fish eye across the bottom of the bowl. I looked up at Mrs. Cantanker, my heart pounding. She was staring at me, a sly glimmer in the depths of her gaze.

I returned my attention to the bowl . . . and then I saw it, high in the rafters—a small, crouched shape. I caught the vague outline of an arm, a leg, all diaphanous, as if made of the most delicate gray mist. The figure wasn't moving. It looked as if it were hiding.

"It's in the corner," I said, in an awed little whisper. "Up there. It's very still."

"Hah!" Mrs. Cantanker exclaimed. "Charlatan! I knew it!" She swept toward me, suddenly terrifying and huge, her mouth stretched into a rictus grin. "There is no spirit in this room. They cannot get past the wards of the High Blackbird's study. You did well until now. Wearing the young mistress's clothes, trying to make us all think you *belonged* in fine silks and ribbons. But I told you there'd be no fooling me."

"What?" I looked back into the water in a panic. What was she saying? The spirit was still there in the rafters. But it was no longer immobile. It was drifting, curling like a thread of smoke among the beams. It was a girl.

Mrs. Cantanker gripped my wrist and twisted it

cruelly, dragging me toward the door. "Mr. Grenouille, she is an imposter. I'm sure you tried your best, but she is not who we were searching for. I suggest we throw her out, or take her to the Vine Room, which is still an excellent option—"

All at once a light bulb in the wall, encased in a metal cage, flared red, washing the room in a glaring, bloody light. Mrs. Cantanker froze.

Mr. Grenouille squeaked. "The spirit lamp," he whispered. "Ysabeau . . . there *is* something here."

I wrenched myself from Mrs. Cantanker's grasp and stumbled back to the bowl. The girl in the rafters was growing clearer by the second. I saw a pair of eyes materialize, glowing like twin moons. Then the hint of a beautiful gown and strands of golden hair, all of it moving slowly, as if underwater . . .

"That isn't possible," Mrs. Cantanker hissed, staring around the room. "They can*not* get in!"

She raced to the desk and jerked open a drawer, hurling a handful of salt into the air. Then she ran for the dish, her hands gripping its edges as she stared into it. I knew at once she couldn't see the girl in the rafters. Whereas *I* had just realized I could see the ghost, dish or no. She was writhing, stretching down toward us. Toward *me*.

"*Kaithus!*" Mrs. Cantanker bellowed. "Kaithus mihalit!"

The shape recoiled, her hair flaring out behind her. I thought I recognized her face. Green eyes, like pine needles.

Then it was over. The red lamp extinguished. The dish of water overturned, and silvery liquid flooded silently across the desk. Mrs. Cantanker looked at me, breathless. Mr. Grenouille extricated himself from the drapes with whose help he had tried to make himself invisible. "Is it gone?" he whispered. "Are we safe?"

"Safe?" Mrs. Cantanker practically shouted. She strode across the room, scanning the ceiling with a jewel-lensed pair of opera glasses. "A spirit got into the High Blackbird's study. Of course we're not *safe*."

"But there are spirits everywhere in the house," Mr. Grenouille said. "What does it—"

"There are no spirits in *this* part of the house!" Mrs. Cantanker roared, and Mr. Grenouille flinched so violently I worried he'd thrown out his back. "The old inhabitants know well not to enter here, and no new ones can get past the wards in Pragast Wood." She wheeled about to face me. "What are you playing at, hmm? What have you smuggled in under all that mangy hair?"

"I didn't bring anything with me," I snapped. "You told me to find the spirit and I did, so I don't see why you're angry with me."

Mrs. Cantanker glared at me. I glared back. Seeing a ghost should be a momentous occasion in anyone's life, but Mrs. Cantanker had managed to ruin it entirely. I was about to tell her what I thought of her when Mr. Grenouille stepped between us.

"Well, whatever it is, it's gone now," he said. And then his weak little face began to beam, and he threw up his hands in a cheer. "There can be no doubt now! *You,* Miss

Zita, are a Blackbird. Oh, your mother would be so proud. And to think she missed you by such a small margin. . . ."

His words cut through the haze of my anger. I thought of the blurry figure from my deepest dreams, a sweet voice, and the scent of violets and rosemary.

"When did she die?" I whispered.

"Just a few months ago! Not long. Not long at all."

Just a few months . . . To think that all this time I'd *had* a mother and a family, that if only the scarecrow had walked faster and the letter had arrived sooner I might have been welcomed home as a daughter instead of a legal term in a sheaf of papers.

Or you'd be dead too, I thought. *Frozen over your dinner and dripping stone from the end of your nose, and* your *ghost flitting about in the rafters.*

"What happened to me?" I asked. We were back in the morning room, Mrs. Cantanker, Mr. Grenouille, and me, seated in front of the windows and watching the sun skim in a slow arc across the tops of the trees.

"Why was I only found now, after they'd died?"

Mr. Grenouille's face sagged. "I'm sorry about that," he said. "I spent the last ten years searching for you, up mountains and down rivers, into woods and deep caves. I've been everywhere, followed every lead. But every road ended in failure, and with every passing year, my hope dwindled. Were you kidnapped? Lost? Dead? No one had the slightest idea. All we knew was that on the fourth of March, in the Year of the Wild Boar, you vanished."

Vanished? But why? Who had left me, covered in soot and my hair full of twigs, on the orphanage doorstep? I wished I could remember. Something had happened, something in between my life as the beloved daughter and my life as an orphan. But what?

Mrs. Cantanker swirled her tea and made a small, bored *tch* with her tongue, as if settling herself in for a tale she had heard many times before. Mr. Grenouille's gaze turned to the window. "You were still so small then, barely two winters old," he said. "You'd gone out to play in the garden with your little dog. I was with your mother in the study, drawing up some papers. We heard you laughing, and the pup barking. And then all went quiet. A nanny saw you walking toward the woods a few minutes past three o'clock, your hand outstretched as if someone was just ahead. But she swore there was no one there."

I shuddered. I couldn't remember any of this. My memories began at the orphanage, where I woke up cold in the morning and went to bed filthy and tired from working the enormous, clanking, wool-spinning machines. It made me feel odd, hearing of nannies and castles and witches. It sounded like the story of a different girl, someone exceptionally interesting, not Mrs. Boliver's maid.

"We turned this world inside out in search of you," Mr. Grenouille continued. "And the next world too. We sent out affidavits into the spirit realm, swore terrible revenge on any dead thing that did not accommodate the search. We did not find so much as a shoe or button. Not a *single* sign pointed to where you might have gone. It was as if you had vanished into thin air."

"It was very sad to see," Mrs. Cantanker murmured. "Your poor father . . . driven to distraction with grief. He died in a shipwreck six years ago, on his way to fumigate a haunted wood. But I suppose one saves oneself all sorts of trouble by dying."

I frowned at her, but the words caused a memory to bloom in my mind: firelight, the smell of oak and tobacco, me sitting on someone's knee, someone very tall and wearing a scratchy coat. *Papa?*

"And your mother . . . ," Mr. Grenouille said in a trembling little voice. "Georgina never stopped looking. She believed your disappearance to be an act of revenge, planned by some dead thing. I tend to agree. The Brydgeborn family has battled many horrible creatures over the centuries. They have disturbed things deep in the spirit realm, things that do not forget and do not forgive. One of them might have hidden you away with some spell, shielding you from all our powers of detection."

"But you did find me," I said. "Eventually."

"And entirely by accident!" Mr. Grenouille exclaimed delightedly, though he took one look at my blank, sad face and deflated again. "A tip came in from beyond the veil, a letter written in some nasty, sticky ink, saying to look for you in Cricktown. Now, as you can imagine, I fed a scarecrow a drop of Brydgeborn blood, wound a lock of hair from your childhood through its rib cage, and sent it there at once. Three weeks later, it returned with news that it had delivered the letter to the owner of the lock of hair, Miss Zita Brydgeborn herself! I don't know if I believed it. I don't know if *you* believed it. Perhaps we'd all given up on each other by then. But as I waited for you to arrive, I became rather certain it *was* you. . . ."

Mr. Grenouille took my hand, his little eyes searching my face. "I'm sorry it took so long," he said. "But you're here now. You're alive. You must be very careful, Zita. Whatever came for you all those years ago, whatever killed your family, may well still be lurking nearby. You must begin your training at once."

I pulled my hand away. The room felt suddenly stuffy,

as if it were full of people I could not see, all peering over my shoulder and breathing down my neck. I looked out the window, across the garden to where the woods rose sharp and dark against the flat white sky. They seemed familiar for a moment, as if I'd sat here before, looking upon this exact view.

My dog's name was Teenzy, short for Tintinnabulum. . . . I was out in the garden when my old life ended.

An image flashed across my mind: something tall and thin standing just inside the shadow of the woods, and me in my white pinafore, dwarfed by those vaulting trees, a pale smudge against the dark. A little black dog was growling behind my ankles. We were watching the figure sway, one long arm outstretched toward us but never touching the light.

The figure in the woods sang to me in a voice like winter, like black water stirred suddenly by a ripple. I'd started toward it curiously. Teenzy had barked, shrill and desperate. And then all had fallen still.

The snapping of buckles from Mr. Grenouille's

briefcase brought me to my senses. He was moving briskly, spreading papers across a cluttered writing desk, procuring a bottle of fine blue ink and a poppy-colored quill.

"Come, Zita. Sign here. It's almost midday, and I really don't want to trouble you any longer than is absolutely necessary."

It occurred to me that we must be quite an unpleasant family to deal with, and Mr. Grenouille no doubt wanted to see the end of the matter.

I sat down at the desk and picked up the quill. I scanned the lines of the document quickly, catching words such as "bequeathed," "woods," "castle and outbuildings," "accounts."

It may seem that I had no choice at all in that moment, that the decision was an obvious one, but I hesitated all the same. *"A true Blackbird is graced with cunning, sly wits, a sharp tongue, and the power to repel the evils of night and fog. But! In return, they bear a great burden and are feared by both the living and the dead."*

So it *was* a crossroads for me, a gallows towering over it and a hawthorn tree hunched at its edge. I could go back to Cricktown, dust and polish for the rest of my life, listen to the radio box tell the weather while Mrs. Boliver exclaimed, "Rain! Rain on Wednesday! Oh, my joints." And then I could fade away, peaceful as you like, an old woman who'd never caused any trouble, never witnessed anything too dreadful, and never done anything too terrible or too good.

Mr. Grenouille smiled at me encouragingly.

Mrs. Cantanker pinched her mouth into a thin, bloodless line.

I dipped the quill, and very carefully, making sure I did not wobble or place a single letter wrong, I wrote my name on the paper.

Chapter Five

JUST like that I went from being a penniless housemaid to the mistress of Blackbird Castle, Pragast Wood, and several desolate mountain peaks, as well as a bank vault in Manzemir in which resided hundreds of thousands of gold galleons and, according to Mr. Grenouille, a unicorn horn and several priceless medallions stolen from the seventh circle of hell. But to me, being a sentimental creature, the greatest gift was my name.

With a few splatters of ink, I had become part of something. I had been given roots and history, a place in a family that did good and battled the darknesses of the world. I wasn't sure yet whether I deserved that place. I wasn't sure I belonged in this castle, with its grand spires and peaked roofs, and its hundreds of magic-drenched rooms. I felt I still had to prove myself, and that Blackbird Castle was waiting for me to do so. But I *was* a witch, and with the sudden flood of certainty that accompanied this knowledge, I felt capable of anything.

"Well," said Mrs. Cantanker as we stood facing each other in the entrance hall. Mr. Grenouille had departed, whistling away through the gardens and down the wooded path into the valley. "I suppose you're to be a Blackbird, then."

"I suppose so," I said, trying not to grin ear to ear.

Mrs. Cantanker frowned. And then her expression shifted, and suddenly it was no longer cruel or haughty. It was weary and resigned, a look that said, *I am tired, and this is not what I want for my life, but I am determined to do my best.* I had worn that expression myself on many a grim morning at Mrs. Boliver's, when the floorboards froze my feet and I'd not gotten half the sleep I would have liked. It was a look I could respect.

"I will remain here as your guardian," she said, clasping her hands in front of her. "I will supervise your education and prepare you as best I can for the life of a Blackbird. Your mother would have wanted that."

"Thank you," I said. "I'm awfully grateful—"

"I have no need for your gratitude," she snapped, and whatever sympathy I'd kindled for her went out in a puff of smoke. "You're the most unfit Blackbird ever to set foot in this house. Years behind in your training, gawky, ungainly, unrefined. But you're all we have, and life does like to play its little jokes. . . . You'll attend lessons every day. You're to come down to breakfast at the bell and eat dinner with me in the Amber Room at seven. And keep away from the servants. They're superstitious villagers and will have nothing good to tell you." She eyed me up and down, her gaze seeming to pick me apart like a bit of roast beef. "Oh, and we'll have to do something about that hair. You look like a paintbrush."

Better than looking like a great big bully, I thought, fighting the urge to shrink into my collar. Plenty of people had made fun of me at the orphanage—for my hair, and my awkward height, and my penchant for keeping small animals under my bed. And not just the other children. The nuns had too, and Mrs. Boliver, and the insults always felt worse coming from grown-ups, because it made one realize that no one ever changed much or became much better.

But I was not going to give Mrs. Cantanker the satisfaction of seeing her words hit their mark. Instead I mustered all my courage and said, "I know I'm not what you were expecting. I'm not beautiful or clever, and I'm not a proper Blackbird. But I'll work hard. I always have. And I . . ." I swallowed. "I *will* associate with the servants. They've been much kinder to me then you've been."

We stood staring at each other across the checkerboard floor, and for a moment I was sure she was going to slap me. But in the end she simply nodded slowly and

I nodded back, and we parted not as friends—not even remotely—but perhaps as a little closer to equals.

As soon as Mrs. Cantanker was out of sight, I burst into a run, galloping all the way back to my room. I closed the door and leaned against it, taking a deep breath. Then I screeched with delight and kicked off my shoes, lying flat on my back on the great fur in front of the fireplace. I stared up at the ceiling, my sumptuous dress spread around me, admiring the dark beams and paintings of sky and trees and winged creatures. The white fur against my neck was springy as a cloud, and I wondered what strange animal had lost its life to make the rug.

My mind began to wander, darting from thought to thought. I wondered if the Brydgeborns had hunted in other lands than these, if they had traveled to the spirit realm and traversed it in carriages and boats. . . .

After a while, I rose and lit a candle with the flint box on the mantel. Then I set to exploring every nook and cranny of my new domain.

I could tell all sorts of things about Greta simply by digging about in her closet. Everything was arranged just so at the front, but in the back was an enormous mess of piled-up dresses and empty candy tins, shoes with no partners, coats with no buttons, and an old stuffed rabbit in a faded dress that looked as if someone had spent years chewing on one arm in particular. I knew that meant it was very well loved indeed.

Everything else in the room had been scrupulously cleaned. The drawers in the nightstand had been emptied. Even the floor under the bed had been swept and polished, and all of the pictures seemed to have been exchanged for new ones. I could see where the old ones had hung, the faded squares on the wallpaper much larger than the nondescript landscapes hanging there now. I dug about under the mattress, hoping for some further hint as to who Greta had been. All I found were several novels and a list tucked between the headboard and the wall.

Read Cavendish's Compendium of Spirits, *chapter nine*

Find pearl earring

Tell John about suspicions

"Well?" said a voice, and I almost leaped out of my skin. I whirled, expecting to see someone in the room. But there was no one.

"Hello?" I said, turning a full circle. The pictures, the closet standing open, a marble bust of a rather irritable-looking gentleman in a tricorn hat—

"I said, 'Well?' Not hello," the voice snapped, and I whirled again, still utterly confused. The voice had a very clipped, no-nonsense tone to it, and it also sounded chilly and echo-y, as if the speaker were standing at the end of a long glass tube.

My eyes alighted once more on the marble bust. I crept toward it slowly. And then its stone eyebrows raised, and its mouth quirked, and it glared at me.

"As in, 'Well, what are you going to do about your family, which is currently cursed to eternal petrification down in the dining room?'"

I flinched. Then I circled the bust, examining it for

strings or wires. "Who are you?" I asked, eyeing its tricorn hat and mustache.

"I am a marble bust. But I *used* to be a Telurian prince. My spirit was bound to this effigy one hundred and fourteen years ago, when I angered one of the twelve kings of the underworld. I was forced to flee, and now I am doomed to cling to it for all eternity, or at least until I feel very confident the king is not going to find me and devour my soul, which I don't think will be any time soon. Anyway, I asked you a question."

"I don't know what I'm going to do," I said, coming back around to face the marble prince. "I don't understand what's going on."

"Well, I can tell you one thing: languishing about on a fur rug and staring at the ceiling is not the path to enlightenment."

"I know *that*," I said. "But I only just got here, and I know hardly anything about being a witch—"

"Excuses," he said. "How d'you suppose you'll learn?

By pretending! By pretending so convincingly that you trick yourself and everyone else into believing it. Because in the end, we're all only pretending to be the things people think we are, or pretending to be something else, or looking like a marble bust, when really we're not a marble bust at all."

I stared at the prince, waiting for him to get to the point.

"You must break the curse," he said finally. "You must bring your family back to life and catch their murderer. I see no other solution."

"Do you know who killed them?" I asked hopefully. "Mrs. Cantanker said it was a ghost—"

"I'm a marble head confined to my pedestal. I don't know anything."

"Then how do you know they're dead in the first place?"

"Because sometimes people whisper things in my general vicinity. And just the other day, oh, did I hear some exciting whispers . . . I did indeed! About a spell called ephinadym mulsion. About how the last Blackbird was going to be put in this very room for safekeeping."

"You mean for sleeping."

"I mean for safekeeping. That's you, I suppose. The last Blackbird . . . hmm. Not much like your mother, are you?"

I squinted at the prince. "Did you know her?"

"Alas, I did not. I did not even have the honor of seeing her. My eyes are marble. They gather no light. But I heard her from time to time. . . ." The prince's tone became dreamy. "Her voice was always so beautiful, like the song of a nightingale, or the wind in a rosebush. Your voice is not beautiful at all."

"Oh," I said.

"Yes, it sounds like a dog chewing a stick. Now, as I was saying. Talk to the servants. They *are* an intriguing lot. Make friends with them. And ask them if they know anything about a certain something called the League of the Blue Spider, and a certain witch named Magdeboor. See what they say."

I thought about that. "And what about the curse? Do you know how I can break it?"

"I haven't the foggiest," said the marble prince. "Now go! Shoo! Be gone!"

"This is *my* room—" I started to say, but the marble prince dismissed me with a shake of his head. "I was here long before you, young lady," he said, and began to reminisce about distant times as if I weren't there at all, about how he had once played cards with the Tentacle King of Dreng and not exactly won, but at least lost very heroically. In the end I put one of Greta's petticoats over his head and turned him to face the wall. Then I set off in search of answers.

I found Bram in a dusty corridor, balancing on a chair and attempting to stuff a crack in the cornice with straw.

"Mice?" I asked, stopping next to him.

Bram shook his head. "Triggles," he said, gritting his teeth. "Little wretches. I patch up one of their passageways, and they dig a dozen more."

I wanted to ask him what triggles were, but I also

didn't want to seem stupid, so I did the logical thing and assumed they were pests at least tangentially related to mice. "Have you tried tea leaves from the bottom of the pot?" I suggested. "At Mrs. Boliver's, where I used to work, I'd scrape them up and plop them all over the shelves in the pantry to keep the crawlies out. Worked like a charm."

Bram gave me a confused glance and began stuffing another of the little doorways. I turned red.

"Look, I'll help you," I said quickly, dragging over a second chair. Hitching up my skirts, I climbed onto it. Bram looked at me as if I were mad, but I didn't stop. I began snatching handfuls of straw from the bucket in the crook of his arm, stuffing them into the popped-out eye socket of a plaster cherub. The straw smelled stingingly of lavender oil, as if it had been drenched in the stuff.

"Bram?" I said, after a while. "Have you ever heard of something called the League of the Blue Spider?"

Bram wobbled on his chair. "What do you know of that?"

"Nothing," I said. "That's why I'm asking."

I was pleased to note that while he had been shocked by my question, he did not look entirely unhappy. If anything, the little rain cloud under which he seemed to be operating lifted slightly. But in the end he only returned to his bucket, saying quietly, "I can't speak of them. It isn't allowed."

"Why not?"

"Because. Terrible things will happen."

"You know, terrible things mostly happen when people *don't* speak of things. It's almost always better in the long run to say things rather than to not say things."

I didn't know if this was true, but the Mother Superior had always told us that when she wanted us to confess to something, and I *very* much wanted to know whatever Bram knew of the League of the Blue Spider. I thought I'd try my luck.

"It's not that simple," said Bram. "Not in this house. I would *like* to tell you, but—"

I remembered Minnifer's mouth clamping shut, her eyes

swiveling desperately. Were Bram and Minnifer under some sort of enchantment too? But why? And who had cast it?

"What if you don't tell me?" I said. "What if you *showed* me? Where is Minnifer?"

"Mrs. Cantanker gave her fifty-seven pillowcases to mend," said Bram. He hopped off his chair and peered up at me gently. "I'm sorry. And thank you for helping me. It was very nice of you."

Casting one last tragic look at the tufts of straw in the ceiling, he headed down the corridor, his bucket banging against his leg.

I continued to stand on my chair, feeling a bit foolish. Then I sighed, dragged the chair back to the spot where it had no doubt stood for decades, and returned to my room.

I was eager to talk to the marble prince again, but when I removed the petticoat from his head, I found him cold and immobile, his mouth shut tight. His expression had changed: the haughtiness was gone from his brow, and his sneering lips were turned down. He looked as if he had been frightened quite badly, and then frozen that way.

"What happened here?" I said.

I tried asking him careful questions, using just the right words. "The League of the Blue Spider," I whispered. "Ephinadym mulsion." But the prince's lips remained resolutely closed.

What a strange place I've stumbled into, I thought, and set off to explore the castle on my own.

I'd not gone very far, only down the corridor and into a chamber mostly occupied by a large, leafy tree, when Minnifer poked her head in like a small, lively owl.

"Bram said you wanted a tour?" she said, and I whirled so quickly I almost lost my balance. Bram stood in the doorway too, his hands in his pockets.

"I'd love a tour," I said, trying to regain my composure. "But don't you have fifty-seven pillowcases to mend?"

"Yes," said Minnifer. "Mrs. Cantanker likes to keep

us busy. Says it keeps us out of mischief. But she also sends the triggles down each night to undo the work I've done, so she can't be in any great hurry to have them finished. We'll be fine unless she catches us. And she won't. She doesn't know the castle the way we do."

Minnifer winked at me, and I smiled back, following her into the corridor. "What's the matter with her anyway?" I asked. "What did anyone ever do to her that she acts like she's got a load of hedgehogs stuffed down her—"

"Shhh," said Minnifer, giggling and casting an anxious look down the corridor. "She failed her tests, you know. . . . She's an underwitch and always will be. Quite the grandest society lady, but that counts for figs in the world of witches."

"She's not even a real witch?" I asked.

"Well, not the way your mother was," said Minnifer, suddenly serious. "But don't let it fool you. She's studied all sorts of things, visited all sorts of mad folk. She's interested in the dark arts, that one. You underestimate her for one second and she'll eat you alive."

I gulped. Minnifer took a candlestick from a side table and lit it. "But who cares about Mrs. Cantanker? She's probably soaking in a tub somewhere with cucumbers over her eyes, and *we've* got a castle to explore."

She snatched my arm, and the three of us hurried down the corridor in a little bouncing globe of light, tallow and smoke streaming behind us like a pennant.

"Shall we start in the Library of Souls?" said Minnifer, her voice echoing as we went down the dragon staircase. "Start with a bang?"

"Start with us all getting eaten, you mean," said Bram. "I saw the bulldogs in there just this morning."

"Oh," said Minnifer, casting a sidelong look at me. "The spirits of seventeen bulldogs covered in horrible warts. Very unfriendly. Origins unknown. Yes, perhaps not. The Orchid Room, then! That's a lovely one, and the orchid wallpaper hasn't driven anyone mad in *ages*."

"I say we start in the west wing and work our way east," said Bram. "That way we'll be well past all the really horrible corners by nightfall." He cast a meaningful glance at Minnifer. "And Zita will see *all* the things she needs to."

Chapter Six

NOTHING is quite as it seems.

That was the first thing I learned about witches' houses. Gilt mirrors opened into corridors, long as train carriages and glittering with gas lamps. Walls folded about with the pull of a brass lever, turning a perfectly respectable-looking parlor to a potion kitchen. Some rooms had groves of mushrooms growing between the tiles, watered by little pewter pipes, and in one gallery, a staircase ran upside down across the ceiling. "For the Bellamy ghost," said Bram, as if that explained everything.

I saw the ghost in question—a large man in

old-fashioned pantaloons and a red velvet coat, sitting on the upside-down stairs, chin in hands, peering at us mournfully. I shivered.

"The house really *is* full of spirits," I murmured, remembering Mr. Grenouille's words.

"Oh, yes," said Minnifer. "Hundreds upon hundreds. It's a sanctuary for them. It's not really legal to keep ghosts from passing on, but the ones who would cause more trouble in the lands of the dead, or the ones that have been expelled for political reasons . . . those are the ones Georgina allows to stay. Most witch families will banish all ghosts right away, but we were never *that* sort of house."

"*Most* witch families?" I squinted at Minnifer. "I thought Mrs. Cantanker said the Brydgeborns were the last of the reigning witch families," I said. "Are there others?"

"A handful," said Minnifer, as we inched around a gaping hole in the floor. I peeked over its edge and saw all the way down to the cellars and up to the sky high above.

It was as if someone had dropped an anvil on the house. "There're the Bluejays of Manzemir, the Jelossians of Belaru, the Balaikabaradas of Rajan. . . ." Minnifer began to count on her fingers, then gave up with a dismissive gesture, saying, "But most of them are just regular high-society folk these days. Not worth the shoes they walk in, that's what Georgina used to say. In the old days, they'd band together when there was a larger breach and work to banish the soul eaters that came pouring into the lands of the living. They would have proper battles with ranks of witches marching across the fields. But I suppose they don't have time to fight the darkness anymore, what with all the feasts they've got to attend and assemblies they've got to speak at. I think most of them wouldn't know a moorwhistler if it bit them on the nose."

I wouldn't know a moorwhistler if it bit me on the nose either, but it alarmed me that those whose *business* it was to know these things were just as ignorant. If the dead were indeed as terrible as I had begun to imagine, and if one had just cursed my family to eternal petrification, all these half-retired witches should be very worried indeed.

We entered a greenhouse, the air muggy, bizarre plants growing wild and untamed all the way to the leaded-glass cupola. Bram and Minnifer began to argue quietly, about what I wasn't sure. I sometimes wondered if they were brother and sister, though they didn't look alike and they certainly didn't act alike. Minnifer had a rather merciless streak beneath all her giggling, and Bram, though he had seemed very serious and particular about everything at first, was patient and long-suffering. He kept busy telling Minnifer what to do, and Minnifer kept busy ignoring him.

I was only half listening to them, my gaze following the twisting stems and fanlike leaves, noxious purple blossoms and jewel-bright fruits. I found myself looking up at a ring of stained-glass ravens unfolding along the perimeter of the cupola, their wing tips touching, as if cut from paper.

"Why is it called Blackbird Castle?" I asked, as we passed under a plant whose blossoms were shaped like bright pink babies with little hands and sly faces.

"Ah, that's a tale," said Minnifer. "It was Magdeboor who named it."

My skin prickled at the mention of that name. *"Ask them . . . about Magdeboor. See what they say."*

"But not the bad Magdeboor, not the Magdeboor everyone whispers about," said Minnifer. "This was the first Magdeboor, Mary Coalblood, the very first Brydgeborn." And puffing herself up like an actress on a stage, Minnifer began her story.

"Long ago, before there were witches, before the first Magdeboor ever planted the seedlings that became Pragast Wood, this hill was a sacred burial place. Blackbirds nested here, crows and ravens and jackdaws swirling around it like smoke from dusk till dawn. It was thought their wings bore souls safely across the river and into the underworld. People came from far and wide with their dead. They brought them up the mountainside and left them in the grass. And then the birds swarmed. . . ."

Minnifer shuddered and clutched the candelabra,

and we all huddled slightly closer together as we passed beneath the drooping vines. "The trouble began when Magdeboor had the first castle built. It wasn't much of a castle, more of a tower with two windows. But after she built it, all the birds went away. Perhaps they didn't like the sound of the stonemasons, or perhaps Magdeboor asked them to leave because they were annoying her. Whatever the case, they all vanished into the sky, and that was that. You'd think no one would have minded, but *everyone* did. The peasants were furious. Because the peasants were furious, the king became furious too. So one day, the king climbed up the mountain and confronted Magdeboor.

"'What will happen to us now?' he demanded. 'The birds are gone! The villagers fear their souls will no longer cross over!'

"And Magdeboor, her students and daughters standing silently behind her, clad all in black, like tar and storm clouds, said, 'We will be your blackbirds. We will be your ravens and crows and jackdaws, your dark wings and messengers. We will shepherd your souls to safety.' That was the first Magdeboor," said Minnifer darkly. "She was the good one."

We had arrived in a high, dim gallery. Part of the roof was caving in and long strands of yellow light trailed down, pooling on the parquet floor. Every inch of the walls was covered with ornately framed pictures, except where two or three were missing, like gaps in a toothy smile.

The pictures showed landscapes, or ladies and gentlemen in stylish hats and capes eating dinner, or writing books, or looking thoughtfully into the distance while stabbing strange beasts with silver scissors. Cats, tawny rabbits, or crows, lurked in the backgrounds, glinty-eyed and mysterious. One of the largest pictures showed a witch in an angular black dress shaped like an umbrella. She looked no older than twenty. Like me, her hair was a wild tangle, her face a bit surly. She was striding confidently deeper into the picture, but looking back over her shoulder at the viewer. In one hand she held a gold coin, in the other a sprig of lavender.

"But there were other Magdeboors," said Minnifer quietly. She did not look at the girl in the painting.

"Who is that?" I asked, approaching the portrait. It was much larger than the others. A curled-up cat lurked in its darkened background, along with a scroll with foreign writing on it, a half-eaten apple, and a skull on a table. And even farther back, deep within the layers of paint and oil, a figure, thin as a wisp of smoke. It was very tall. Its arms were unnaturally long, hanging almost to its feet.

I knew who it was. I had met it once, years ago, at the edge of the woods.

"Magdeboor III," said Bram, squinting up at the girl in the umbrella dress. "Also known as the Dark Queen. Also known as Mad Magdeboor Brydgeborn. Also known as . . . are you all right?"

I must have shuddered, because both Minnifer and Bram were looking at me curiously.

"I'm fine," I said, still staring at the wispy figure in

the background. It was the merest suggestion of a thing, hardly there at all. But looking at it gave me a horrible sinking feeling. Once again I saw the soaring trees, a pale hand extending toward me. What was that creature doing in a painting of my ancestor?

"What happened to her?" I asked. "Why did they call her mad?"

"Because she was," said Minnifer. "A proper witch will watch over the boundaries of life and death, ferry lost souls into the lands of the dead, and keep the moorwhistlers and fangores and red dukes from devouring them along the way. But Magdeboor wasn't good at any of those things the way other witches were, and she became terribly envious. She also became rather friendlier with the moorwhistlers than with her own sisters, and she was even known to nibble a soul or two in her day."

The three of us stood in a pool of light, looking up at the painting. Bram made a disgusted face. I remembered the coachman and his talk of eating hearts on beds of boiled greens.

"She would go wandering in the lands of the dead for weeks at a time, exploring the woods and marshes," Minnifer continued. "And eventually she went too deep, all the way down to the underworld. She brought something back with her. Normal folk bring back a spoon or a tea towel from their travels, but *Magdeboor* brought back one of the high-ranking dead. It whispered in her ear and made her quite evil.

"She began to think life was not half as interesting as people made it out to be, and people were just bags of meat, not really worth the trouble. She wreaked havoc on the villages and graveyards, kidnapped children and ate their souls, and once she inherited this castle, she threw out all the other Blackbirds and began filling it up like one of those old-fashioned witches of yore, with skulls, and blood in bottles, and doorways to other places. And it wasn't where things were headed. Witches were becoming modern and government approved. They were being given positions at court and invited to banquets. And Magdeboor disagreed with all that. She thought, *Why should we bow to powerful men and cruel governments and all the people who used to burn us at the stake? Why not fight them tooth and claw, and eat their souls for breakfast?"*

"Well, that's not unreasonable," I said. "Except for the breakfast bit."

"Of course it's not *unreasonable*," said Minnifer. "But it is very stupid. Supposing all the elephants in the zoo decided to trample the people who came to feed them. It wouldn't be unreasonable, because who wants to be locked up in a zoo? But it's stupid, because you're still in a cage, surrounded by people, only no one likes you anymore or brings you peanuts."

Minnifer crossed the gallery. Bram and I followed, and we all paused beneath a diamond-paned window. Shrouds of ivy grew against the glass, turning the light green and slithering, as if we were underwater.

"You've got to be clever about changing the rules," said Minnifer. "And Magdeboor wasn't. She wanted to change everything at once, and by change everything, I mean conquer the world with an army of the dead and feast on the souls of the living. She probably would have done it, too, if the other witches hadn't caught wind of it. They banded together to bind her essence in the underworld. They burned her alive, right there."

Minnifer pointed out the window. Across the court, through the dancing leaves, I saw the looming black carcass of the castle's burned wing. Branches of laurel and rhododendron had softened its charred edges and wrapped it in a gentle embrace. But it was a dead, desolate-looking place, and the ivy that poured from its broken windows and crawled across the buttresses looked like nothing so much as thick black smoke.

"What a horrible way to die," I said. "To know that your whole family has turned against you and wants you gone."

"Yes," said Minnifer. "But she deserved it. You know, they didn't even bury her in the family plot. They put her just outside it, in Pragast Wood. You passed it on the way in. The great big mausoleum? That's hers."

"Awful place," said Bram. "Gives me the shivers just thinking about it."

We continued down the gallery, peering up at the pictures all around us. I searched for my mother's face or Greta's, but I couldn't find them. No one here looked like me, no one except the wicked Magdeboor. These people were all elegant and hawk-nosed. Their hair was smooth as black oil, their expressions clever or politely bored. I was sure none of them had ever been called gawky or ungainly in their life.

I thought of Greta down in the dining room. She didn't look like a Blackbird either, but she did look lovely, golden-haired and fashionable. I imagined her wearing the expensive clothes in her closet, marching through the house and brilliantly doing battle against the evils of night and fog. I was no Greta. I wondered if that was why Mrs. Cantanker disliked me so, and I wondered if my mother might have liked Greta more too, perhaps not at once, but with time. . . .

I shook my head to rid myself of these thoughts and followed Bram and Minnifer toward the end of the gallery and a door with the words ANTECHAMBER OF ETERNAL

DREAMS in gilded script above it. We were just about to pass through it when something caught my eye: an open panel in the wall and, inside, a staircase, quite narrow, winding upward into shadows. There would have been nothing remarkable about it, nothing to set it apart from the dozens of other staircases we had already seen during our explorations—except that every tread, every panel, and every inch of its railing was painted a deep sapphire blue.

"Where do those go?" I asked, pointing.

"Oh!" said Minnifer, startled. "They do creep up on you. . . ." Then she planted herself firmly between me and the blue stairs and said, "You're never to go up there, Zita. *Never.* It's not safe. I know it's a witch's house, so nowhere is safe, but up there . . . really, you mustn't. Those stairs used to lead to the attic in the north wing—"

"Where Magdeboor was killed?"

"And where she was imprisoned in her last days. The stairs were hacked to pieces so that she couldn't escape down them, but when the servants came back after the fire, what did they find? The blue stairs, good as new. It's said they lead straight into the spirit realm now." Minnifer cast them one more mistrustful look. "Anyway, it's the rule that no one climbs them, so you mustn't either. The blue stairs? Utterly, utterly forbidden. Do you understand?"

"Utterly," I said, laughing as Minnifer herded me along the gallery. But as soon as I'd turned my back on the stairs, I felt a chill pass over me, and the strange weight of a gaze. I glanced over my shoulder. Frost glistened on the blue banister, a little patch of winter, as if something had been standing there moments before, the cold flowing off it. I told myself it was just the way the candlelight caught the blue paint, but I wasn't sure.

We left the gallery, moving down corridors and up staircases, their banisters casting long shadows over the damask wallpaper. We passed padlocked doors labeled such things as ROOM OF MARBLE HEADS and VESTIBULE OF BLOOD, and one door that was hardly large enough for a cat called the TINY QUEEN'S THRONE ROOM. We passed the chamber mostly occupied by the large, leafy tree, its branches rustling and whispering inside. And then I saw that stupid crow again, perched on a chandelier high above my head. For a moment I was sure it was a sculpture. But then it screeched and took flight, and vanished out of a partly open window, in a flurry of black feathers.

I shook my head. "I thought all of them had left."

"They had!" said Minnifer. "It's a good omen, that. You arriving, and a crow coming soon after. It means things are about to change."

We ended the tour in the servants' hall, deep in the roots of the castle. It was the warmest place, by far, and the nicest smelling. The bundles of drying lavender filled the air with their pungent fumes. A fire blazed in the huge stone fireplace. When we had finished dinner, we melted an entire block of chocolate into a pan of milk and sat on the floor in front of the hearth to drink it. The wide, polished boards glimmered, warm from the glow of the coals, and we sipped from black china mugs and ate crumbly shortbread in the shape of sickle moons.

It turned out Bram was the cook of all the delicacies I'd had at breakfast, and all of the ones we had just feasted on. He had fashioned tiny amuse-bouches for our supper—buttered sandwiches with salmon florets and cucumber sails and dustings of dill, cherry tomatoes stuffed with savory bread, golden quiches, their fillings lighter than air—and served them on a silver dish. He seemed very proud of himself when I said they were the most delicious things I'd ever eaten.

"He'll be a great chef one day, you wait and see," said Minnifer, and Bram reddened and crunched busily at his shortbread.

"Is that your plan, Bram?" I asked. "Are you going to be a cook? I would go to your shop every day if you sold a-moose-booshes there."

Minnifer laughed at my pronunciation, but I didn't mind.

"Maybe one day," said Bram, picking at a splinter in the floor. And then Bram and Minnifer peered at each other, the same sad, odd look they had exchanged the night before. I glanced between them, feeling suddenly left out.

"Why *did* you stay after what happened?" I asked them. "Not that I'm not very happy you're here, but you're both old enough to work anywhere. Bram could be cooking in any great house or big city—"

"I'm in a great house," said Bram seriously. "The greatest house."

"Yes, but everyone's dead or run away," I said. "And there's dark sorcery afoot, not to mention Mrs. Cantanker—"

"This is our home," said Minnifer. "And anyway, Bram's not allowed to go anywhere without me. We look out for each other, don't we, Bram?"

Bram nodded. Minnifer nodded too, satisfied. "Sometimes," she said, "I think this whole place could go to ruin, and all the witches of the world could be working in offices and sweeping train platforms, and Bram and I would still be here as little old people, tending the rosemary and patching the roof. They took us in, you see, from an orphanage down in the valley. I was seven and Bram was eight, and maybe it doesn't make sense to other people, but . . . it's hard to leave a place you've known so long."

"It wasn't hard for me to leave Cricktown," I said. In fact, it was knowing the place well that had made it easy to say goodbye to its low, peaked roofs and petty people. But then I thought for a moment and added quietly, "I know all about being an orphan, though. I'm glad we all found our way here."

Bram and Minnifer smiled at me. And we sat in our little bubble of warmth and firelight, talking about the life of a servant, counting the calluses on our hands and telling stories about finicky masters and mistresses, until all thoughts of growing old and being orphans were forgotten. We were quite dizzy with the sugar, and being very loud, when a long, low bell sounded through the servants' hall, followed by footsteps, sharp and swift. Bram startled, looking toward the door.

"Quick," he said, leaping to his feet. "This way," and

we ran giggling out of the servants' hall just as Mrs. Cantanker stalked in. She was in a rage, calling our names. We hid behind a curtain in the butler's pantry, holding our breath, and Mrs. Cantanker passed within a few feet of us, poking her nose into the scullery, then the dairy. When she was a good twenty yards off, we dashed down the servants' corridor in a gale of laughter, out of the kitchens and up the stairs. I swear Mrs. Cantanker heard us, but perhaps she thought we were ghosts.

Chapter Seven

LESSONS started at nine o'clock sharp. I woke to find a crisply ironed uniform draped over a chair—a black crepe dress and half cape, black stockings, and a pair of black pointy shoes as shiny as mirrors. A silver bowl, scissors, a bundle of rosemary sprigs, a small bottle of rose water with a brocade puffer, a notebook, a quill, and a birdcage were all arranged carefully around the chair on the floor.

I did not know how these things had arrived or who had brought them, but the room was once again icy, and when I approached the gifts, I saw there were many tiny footprints the size and shape of pumpkin seeds in the frost. They looped here and there over the floor, congregating next to my bed, as if a passel of little creatures had gathered to discuss something. Then the footprints led up the walls and scurried across the ceiling into a hole in the corner.

The triggles, I thought, wondering again what these mysterious beings were. I wasn't sure I liked the idea of anything coming into my room while I was sleeping. But the gifts they had brought were lovely and costly, and whatever reservations I had were soon replaced with excitement.

I washed my face, dressed carefully, and went downstairs to eat breakfast with Minnifer and Bram. Then I set off for the High Blackbird's study, my half cape snug around my shoulders and my many supplies filling my arms and jangling in my pockets. I got lost three times. One staircase ended in a pit of carnivorous flowers. A door I thought I recognized opened only into a tiny square room whose walls and floor and even ceiling were covered with little portraits in gilt frames.

"You know," I muttered at one glaring face, before closing the door again, "if you're going to build a house the size of a small town, there should be road signs and arrows so that regular people can find their way." But I'd given myself plenty of time—I was used to the early mornings of a servant, after all—and I chose the right staircase eventually and climbed up to the tower room with half an hour to spare.

Mrs. Cantanker was seated behind the desk, a pair of elegant glasses on her nose, reading a small brown book whose cover looked suspiciously bloodstained. Her skirts were ruby silk today, and her bejeweled fingers caught the light from the windows and blinked at me like so many judging eyes. I noticed that the family pictures on the High Blackbird's desk had all been removed, the pewter and silver frames replaced with stylish illustrations of yarrow root and sage, sailor's tobacco and fern, beautifully done and utterly academic. Mrs. Cantanker was making her dominion of the place complete.

She glanced up as I entered, her expression surprised, which made me think I looked every inch a witch.

"Good morning," I said brightly, laying down my things carefully on a table. The bottle of rose water landed sideways, rolling toward the edge. I snatched it back just in time and stole a glance at Mrs. Cantanker, bracing myself for insults.

But Mrs. Cantanker only sniffed and tucked her book into a drawer. "I see the triggles delivered the things I ordered?"

"I suppose so," I said. "What are triggles, exactly?"

"Household pets." Mrs. Cantanker rose and approached the table, running a thumb along the sharp edge of the scissors. "Fine stuff, this. A bit too fine."

She turned away and I scowled at her back. And then, out of the corner of my eye, I spotted that crow again. It was perched atop a towering shelf, watching me. I turned all the way around to get a proper look at it. The moment our eyes met, it came swooping down in a whirl of black feathers, heading straight for me. I shrieked and dove under the table. When I peeked out it, my hair disheveled and my mouth agape, the crow had landed on top of the globe, and both it and Mrs. Cantanker were peering at me quizzically.

"It's your bird," said Mrs. Cantanker. "Stop leaping about like an idiot."

"*My* bird?"

"Your animal servant. I was wondering if perhaps it wouldn't come, if the old traditions would forget about you like everyone else had. But here he is! A great big scruffy crow to match your scruffy hair."

Mrs. Cantanker reached out to scratch the bird's head, but it snapped its sharp beak at her and settled belligerently into its feathered ruff. She curled her fingers away, clicking her tongue. "Well! And a temper to match!" She noticed my uncertain expression and rolled her eyes. "Superstitious girl. Look, you might as well know right away that all the tales you've ever heard about witches are lies. It's one great smear campaign, started by some king who didn't want to pay his dues for the fumigation of his woods and palaces. And the common folk lapped it up. They'll call anyone a witch who doesn't do as she's told and has a fondness for graveyards and talking to cats. As for the bird, he's got nothing to do with spirits or demons or all that claptrap they believe in the villages. He's just a helper, bound by the ancient charter of Dindelgorm to serve your family's line. The Brydgeborns tend to have birds. Some witches have rats, or snakes, like in the storybooks. But just as many have beautiful kittens, or dogs, or emerald-shelled turtles."

"What about pointy hats?" I asked. "And broomsticks? Are those just stories too?"

"Broomsticks!" Mrs. Cantanker exclaimed. "A self-respecting witch has no need of brooms, or chalices, or wands, or poppets. Now stop asking questions, and put your bird inside its cage."

I did as I was told, crawling out from under the table and lifting the silver cage. I liked animals quite a lot normally, birds included, but there was something terrifying about a crow up close. I think anyone with an ounce of sense would have reacted the same as I did.

"Here, pretty bird," I whispered, and looked at Mrs. Cantanker questioningly.

"Not like *that*. Name him! Command him!"

I squinted at the crow, which was in the process of stalking across the globe, crushing entire countries under his talons. He almost seemed to be pacing, waiting impatiently for me, and I thought he looked like nothing so much as a bedraggled, somewhat bad-tempered vicar in a winter coat. That's what I'd call him. Vik. Or Vicar. Vikers?

"Here, Vikers!" I called, swinging the cage door invitingly. And then again, louder, "Vikers! Come here at once!"

That did the trick. The bird flew at me, and it was all I could do not to hurl the cage into the air and run screaming from the room. Instead I froze and allowed him to land on my shoulder. He was very heavy. I felt his talons biting through my cape, and for a moment I was sure I was going to shudder violently and send him flapping away again. But then he rubbed his head against my cheek and made a sound almost like a coo. His head was surprisingly soft and warm, his feathers glossy and tinged deepest blue.

"Oh, hello," I whispered. "You're not so bad."

A moment later he slipped into the cage, where he hunched his shoulders and looked straight ahead, very grim and forbidding, as if his work for the day was done and he wanted to be left alone.

I stared at him in wonder. Mrs. Cantanker looked at us both with an expression I was sure was envy.

"What am I supposed to do with him?" I asked, poking a finger through the bars and stroking his head. For a moment he looked annoyed, but then he cooed again and ruffled his feathers, and I couldn't help but smile.

"You'll learn to call him from great distances, speak to him without words, send him on journeys to deliver important messages . . . but not today. Today, he's entirely irrelevant. Close the cage and put him out of your mind."

I did so reluctantly, turning the cage's little key.

Something told me Vikers was a very clever bird and that if he wanted to he could escape quite easily—turn the key himself, or even pick the lock. Vikers seemed to agree, giving me a patient look, as if to say, "We both know this is only a formality and I will leave any time I please."

I nodded at him and winked. Then, once Mrs. Cantanker had instructed me on the proper etiquette of witch uniforms (black buttons only, shoes must be polished *always*, and your hair *must* be in a bun or braid, never loose, because loose hairs are liable to snag, or catch fire, or be used for all sorts of nefarious purposes by spirits and rival witches), the time had come. All through the castle, bells, gongs, and grandfather clocks struck nine o' clock. Mrs. Cantanker positioned me in the center of the room, buffed and brushed, black caped and pointy shoed. And my first lesson as a Brydgeborn Blackbird began.

"A philosopher," said Mrs. Cantanker, stalking across the study, black heels clicking, ruby silks whispering around her ankles, "is one who attempts to capture the truths of the universe so precisely that they become too confusing to understand. A novelist is one who attempts to capture the truths of the universe in such a roundabout way that they become obvious to anyone who reads them."

"And a witch?" I asked, perched on a stool, quill in hand.

"A witch kills the dead."

"Ah," I said, nodding wisely.

"But it's just as necessary," Mrs. Cantanker snapped, as if she suspected I didn't believe her. "In fact, without witches there would be no philosophers, or novelists either. We capture truths as well, though our truths tend to be half rotted and full of teeth and eyeballs. Without us, the foulest creatures of the underworld would have spilled over their borders long ago, devouring souls and spreading fog and darkness across the globe."

This was quite a lot to absorb all at once, but Mrs. Cantanker continued on relentlessly, as if she were discussing geography or the weather. "Most people die and move right along to their final resting place, up or down depending on what sort of life they lived. They're labeled by the appointed authorities, sent off in the right direction, and make the journey without a hitch. But some do not have the necessary accoutrements. Some have unfinished business in the lands of the living. And the longer they're caught in between, the more they begin to . . . change. They forget the shape they had when they were alive. They begin to take on the true shape of their soul, which can be very hideous indeed. A witch's job is to handle anything that comes back. Have you ever seen a denizen of the spirit realm, Zita? Besides the one yesterday?"

"I'm not sure—"

"Straight answers, girl, yes or no. A witch is never unsure."

"All right, no."

"Incorrect," she said, smiling at me rather venomously. "You may not have been *aware* of seeing them. You may only have been aware of a slow chill crawling up your arms, or a scuttling shadow in the corner of your eye. But I assure you, you *have* seen them. Most likely you were simply too uneducated to know it."

I wondered about this, hurtling back through my memories in search of dead faces among the bustle and bright-spotted cheeks of the living. There *had* been that one man in the cellar at the orphanage who never spoke but sometimes rearranged all the jars of pickles and preserves. And then there was whatever had lived atop the boiler in Mrs. Boliver's garden. I had thought it to be a large, unfriendly cat, but it had always been up there, rain or shine, warming its mangy fur as if it were freezing. And then of course the figure in the woods, the figure in the painting of Mad Queen Magdeboor III . . .

"Ah," said Mrs. Cantanker. "You are realizing. Are you disturbed by the breadth of your ignorance? You should be. Spirits are everywhere, in houses and shops, wandering the moors, sitting on lampposts, and leaping from chimney pots like toads. Especially in this day and age, when the influence of the great witch families is diminishing. The borders are left unguarded, gateways untended. More and more spirits linger or come creeping back. There is no fear of the dead in the towns and cities, with their electric light bulbs and gas heating and policemen on every corner. They think they are safe!" She tittered. "But they are simply blind."

I nodded, chewing at the end of my tight new braid and watching Mrs. Cantanker closely. She was very beautiful and clever. I wished she didn't think me such an unworthy creature, because I would have liked to be friends with her.

"You, however, are not allowed to be so ignorant. A Blackbird must see as wide and far as anyone ever has. You must see life and death in all its sordid complexity. You must see what others cannot."

She went to a tasseled cord in the corner and pulled it. A black velvet curtain parted, revealing a painting framed in a tangle of gilt holly and ivy. The painting was very dark, full of curling blue and green shadows. I could just make out two figures standing on a riverbank, offering some tiny glimmering object to the darkness. And on the other side, terrible creatures lurked, angry faced and many armed, claws and snouts and dozens of glaring eyes. The whole scene gave the impression of a nightmare—a vast roiling swath of darkness in which things swam that were not known on earth, in which things sank and were never seen again.

"Here you have it," said Mrs. Cantanker with a flourish. "A Blackbird guiding a spirit into the underworld. Once the spirit's been sent on its way with all the proper equipment and words of encouragement, it's unlikely to come back. But if they have nothing, not even a little light, well . . . The lands of the dead are a dangerous place, full of all manner of monsters. And *all* of them eat souls if they can find them."

She went on like this for some time, telling me about the various responsibilities of a witch, how much one could charge for one's services, and where to buy the best pointy shoes in all of Westval. By eleven o' clock, I had added a tool belt to my heap and several velvet pouches of herbs, each with a tiny brass emblem attached to its drawstring ("So you know which herb is which, even in the dark," Mrs. Cantanker had explained). I'd also been told to read a chapter in an apricot-colored volume that looked suspiciously like a children's book, and been practically drowned in terms and facts, which Mrs. Cantanker threw at me like a cook who has spotted a rat in her kitchen. My head was beginning to feel very full.

". . . and that was when the great witches of old conquered Erasteraf and made it their stronghold," Mrs. Cantanker finished. She put away her brass pointing stick and consulted a pocket watch. "Now. It's almost lunchtime. But before I let you go, I'm going to bring you to a very particular room in the house. The Black Sitting Room. There, you are going to meet a spirit. And you are going to banish it."

I thought of the red lamp flaring, the golden-haired ghost in the rafters. I also thought banishing anything at all sounded well beyond my abilities. But the marble prince had said it was all about pretending, and I wanted

Mrs. Cantanker to think me serene and unflappable, so I nodded capably and followed her to the High Blackbird's desk.

The back of the desk was full of drawers in different shapes and sizes, triangles and circles and rectangles fitted together like puzzle pieces. Each drawer had, instead of a keyhole, a great wobbly eye that swiveled to and fro and followed your every move. Mrs. Cantanker knelt before one such eye—an anxious blue one shot through with red veins—and spoke a very angry word to it. The eye darted about, then closed beneath its wooden lid, and the drawer sprang open. Inside were coins of various sizes, neatly arranged on black velvet. Some were green with verdigris, some rusted, some thick as butter biscuits.

"Every ghost requires safe passage through the Kingdom Between," said Mrs. Cantanker, slipping several coins into a small purple purse. "That is why villagers put coins on the eyes of corpses, or tuck a jewel into an apron pocket or under a tongue. A vial of tears from a loved one or a letter from a sweetheart can also do the trick. But for our purposes, coins are the quickest and most efficient method for sending a ghost on its way."

She handed the purse to me and I took it slowly, knotting it into my belt.

"It seems silly that a ghost should care about money," I said, weighing the purse in my palm. "What's to stop it from wandering into a bank vault and getting all the money it needs? It could buy first-class tickets right through the Kingdom Between!"

"Are you trying to be funny?" Mrs. Cantanker snapped, so coldly I regretted my words at once. "The coins are symbolic. It is the *gesture* the laws of the spirit realm require, not the gold or silver. It is the generosity, the idea that someone in the lands of the living wants a soul to pass into the further veils and was willing to give up the necessary amount. Do you think stolen coins will offer any protection there?"

I shook my head, looking down at my shoes.

"Of course you don't," said Mrs. Cantanker. "Now, as I was saying . . . a coin is only one tool of an educated witch. Name the others mentioned in the chapter you read."

I cleared my throat. "A cross of ash on my forehead will forestall any sort of possession. Rosemary . . ." I thought for a moment. "Rosemary attracts, lavender repels, wormwood cloaks from unwanted attention. Rose petals spark affection in ghosts, and violets inspire overwhelming longing."

"Very good," said Mrs. Cantanker. "And if the spirit attacks?"

"I . . ." My fingers fiddled with the sleeve of my dress. "I don't remember. I don't think it . . ."

Mrs. Cantanker's lips curled upward. "Not to worry! I've been told it's not a particularly *dangerous* spirit."

She glided toward the door and I hurried after her, out of the study and along a narrow corridor squeezed beneath the sloping eaves of the house. Halfway down it, we stopped in front of a plain wooden door.

"Here we are," Mrs. Cantanker said, opening it with a key from her chatelaine. "Yesterday you met a spirit from afar. Now you will meet one in more . . . *snug* quarters."

"Isn't it a bit soon?" I said, not serene and unflappable after all. "It's my first day, and I know hardly anything—"

Mrs. Cantanker's smile widened. "Sometimes, Zita, it is best not to know too much." And before I could open my mouth again, she pushed me into the room and locked the door.

Chapter Eight

AFTER I'd gotten the letter from Mr. Grenouille, I had allowed myself to daydream about long-lost mothers, castles right out of fairy tales, crackling fires, and teetering cliffs of food. Not once had my daydreams involved being locked in a room with a ghost.

The Black Sitting Room was small and stuffy and very, very dark. Its walls and sloping ceiling were paneled in black wood. The chairs were upholstered in black silk. The mantel was draped with a black velvet coverlet, and all the knickknacks and decorations were made of jet or onyx or polished coal. The paintings were so old and dim they looked like black canvases nailed to the wall, though when I peered closely at them, I could just make out the whorled branches of trees barely visible in the paint.

I took several steps into the room, my new shoes squeaking. The air smelled sour, as if the window hadn't been opened in years. Beneath that, I caught the stomach-turning whiff of sickness—oil from unwashed scalps, and the faintest hint of tinctures and peppermint salve for the ill.

I froze, glancing about. *Mrs. Cantanker is just outside. She won't let anything awful happen to me.* But then I recalled her comment about the Vine Room and sending me back to Cricktown in a hatbox, and I gulped.

I turned a full circle, my hands clenched at my sides. Then, with a start, I saw I was not alone. A veiled woman stood in the corner. No breath, no warmth came from her. She added no weight to the room, nothing but a strange loneliness, and even when I looked directly at her, I had the odd impression that I was glimpsing her from afar. Her pale, waxen hands were knotted tightly in front of her. Her eyes, almost invisible behind her black veil, glinted.

I stared at her, my breath escaping in white clouds. The air was suddenly bitterly cold. I saw now that what I had taken for the gleam of velvet was frost, coating the cushions and chairs.

"Give the spirit a coin," Mrs. Cantanker ordered through the door, and I jumped. "Ignore anything it tries to tell you."

I nodded sternly and opened the little purse, eyeing the coins inside. "I suppose you want something so you can cross over?" I whispered to the ghost, choosing a copper farthing and holding it out to her. "Here you are. Go on, ma'am, it's all right!"

The spirit remained motionless. I took a step toward her. Then she twitched and whimpered piteously, and I drew back with a start. My teeth were beginning to chatter, and I could sense the end of my braid freezing where I had chewed on it.

"Not enough," I said to myself. And then louder, for the benefit of Mrs. Cantanker, "I don't think it's enough!"

Mrs. Cantanker *tsk*ed through the door. "Greedy thing. Try one of the pewter coins. Those usually work. They look shiny, but they're quite worthless. Hurry up!"

I *wanted* to hurry up. The ghost was becoming more agitated by the second. She looked back over her shoulder, as if there was something behind her. There wasn't, of course, not that I could see anyway, but then, she wasn't quite here or there. She was partway in-between, and when I squinted, I could just make out a dark landscape stretching away, misty marshes and still waters, and far in the distance, an unwavering red glow.

I held out another coin, a thick pewter one with the face of a saint on it. This one caught the ghost's attention. She seemed to peer at me more closely, though she still seemed a thousand miles away.

"*Zita?*" she said in a thin, dry voice. "*Zita, is that you?*"

I flinched back, staring at her in horror. "You know my name?"

"*Of course I know your name! Oh, child, I have not seen you in such a long time.*"

Mrs. Cantanker rapped sharply on the door. "Do not let it trick you," she said. "Banish it!"

But I could hardly move. The room was cold as winter, cold as the orphanage dormitories in December.

"*I was surprised when they told me you'd survived,*" the spirit said. "*No one ever survives him. Not the Butcher of Beydun.*"

I recovered my poise as best I could and stepped closer to the ghost, lowering my voice so that Mrs. Cantanker could not hear. "How do you know me?" I whispered. "And what do you mean, I survived? Who is the Butcher of Beydun?"

But the ghost wasn't listening. She began to cry, her hands hovering in front of her face.

"*Zita . . . Zita, I have done such terrible things.*"

I wanted to pat her thin, heaving shoulders. I thought

about giving her my handkerchief, but I wasn't sure it would do any good. "It's all right," I said gently. "Whatever you did, I'm sure it's not so bad. We've all done terrible things at one point or another."

"But I've done worse," she wheezed. *"Tell me, child, what is the cost of betrayal? What is the punishment for one who has been disloyal to a family that wished her nothing but good?"*

"I'm . . . not sure," I said. "I'm a bit new to all this, to be honest. But I know that if you take this coin, you'll be able to move on, hopefully someplace nice. Don't cry. Take the coin! Take the whole purse!"

The ghost continued to sob and tremble. *"You would let me go? After all I've done?"*

"Of course!" I said. "There's no point in you staying here. It must get awfully gloomy in this little room, with no one to talk to."

Slowly, her sobs subsided. She took the purse from my hands, her touch so cold and sharp it made my skin sting. *"Thank you, child,"* she whispered. *"Thank you!"*

I smiled halfheartedly, feeling a sudden pang of worry

at giving the ghost a full purse of coins. She bent over it and began counting the money greedily. "If I may ask," I said quickly. "Why do you need such a lot of coins to cross over? What did you do?"

She looked up sharply. *"I was a nanny in this house,"* she said, and suddenly she did not look quite so old and fragile. She was smiling, her yellow teeth crawling with worms and beetles. *"They think I am here because I took all the little golden statues from the Tiny Queen's Throne Room and stashed them at the bottom of my drawer. But I did something much, much worse."*

I gulped. "Wh-what did you do?"

Her black eyes flashed, pinning me with blood-chilling intensity. *"I sold a child to the Butcher King. A child who was my own ward. I built a door of twigs and ivy for him to pass through. I made a path of salt and iron for him to walk on. And then I watched from behind a tree as a little girl in a white dress scampered toward him."*

My head swam. Blood pounded in my ears. "You did that? *You* let him take me away?"

"*Oh, you flatter me, Zitakins, but don't give me all the credit. I was only one small piece in a great big scheme. They want him back, you know. They want the Butcher of Beydun to return, and the Dark Queen with him. And for that they need you. I have no idea how you escaped the first time, how you managed to claw your way out of the darkest depths of the spirit realm. But mark my words, dearie, you will not be so lucky again. He knows you're here. He'll be arriving soon; I heard it on the roads and byways, from the dead near the river. You should not have come back.*"

The spirit was fading, jangling the sack of coins and snickering.

"Wait!" I shouted. "What great scheme? What do you mean?"

The ghost sneered. "*Goodbye, Zita. Let us hope our paths never cross again.*"

She dove at me, and I screamed at the top of my lungs. Mrs. Cantanker flew into the room, her opera glasses held to her eyes and a sachet of petals ready in one hand.

"What happened?" she demanded, peering about. "Is it gone? Did you get rid of it?"

And then she looked at me, standing shocked and purseless, and her face darkened. "Where's your purse? Stupid girl. Did you give it the whole thing?"

I remained mute, my head brimming with questions.

"You did, didn't you? What sort of half-wit gives away an entire purse of coins to a common ghost? And what sort of *witch*—"

She went on like this for some time, but I wasn't listening. I had not been kidnapped all those years ago. I had been sold, bargained away by a wicked nanny for some dark purpose. And then, somehow, I had escaped. *But how?*

We returned to the High Blackbird's study, and as I stood shivering and rubbing warmth back into my hands, I made up my mind. Mrs. Cantanker could call me all the names in her arsenal. She could toss me into haunted chambers to her heart's content. But my family was frozen; Bram and Minnifer were perhaps under some sort of enchantment too; and I was likely on some dead thing's dinner menu. I had work to do, and things to fix, and while I didn't feel at all qualified to fix any of them, all the qualified witches were busy attending feasts and speaking at assemblies.

The day stretched on, the light from the tall windows turning to honey, then amber, then red, and still we were in the study. Mrs. Cantanker screamed at me, making me feel small and foolish. *"Lead*, then *copper*, then *pewter*! If I've said it once, I've said it a thousand times!" I kept my chin up, and I'm proud of that, but there is no satisfaction in seeming something you know you're not. I felt dreadful, and when she at last dismissed me, I went straight to the servants' hall and slouched at the table, pouring out all my troubles to Minnifer and Bram.

Bram was at the stove, presiding over a range of bubbling pots and deliciously steaming pans. He didn't say anything, only raised his eyebrows from time to time and nodded.

Minnifer was much more sympathetic. "Yes, she's not very nice, is she? But Bram made you a lovely supper, and I baked an apricot tart, and if that doesn't cheer you up I'm afraid there's no helping you and you'll have to resign yourself to a life of misery. D'you like apricots?"

"I love apricots."

"I win," said Minnifer, turning to Bram, and Bram sighed.

Bram and Minnifer were always betting about things. "Are you a gambling man?" Minnifer had asked me at breakfast, and I'd said "No," because I wasn't, and she lifted her chin and nodded, like someone who's just observed something puzzling yet deeply interesting. I regretted saying no, because I think she was asking if I wanted to be in on their bets. Would the dough rise or not? Would the specter of the lady above the door to the butler's pantry be friendly today or rude? Would the triggles try to steal anything from the silver cupboard and if so, pitchers or teaspoons? Sometimes Minnifer won and sometimes

Bram won, and then they'd leave something for the other on the table, usually a biscuit, or a ribbon, or a bundle of red berries.

Today, Bram gave Minnifer an extra helping of chocolate mousse with her potatoes and chicken pie, and we all sat down with our plates. We ate heartily, the wind murmuring against the leaded windows like a bitter uninvited guest, occasionally flinging twigs and leaves against the panes. It occurred to me that Mrs. Cantanker was waiting for me in the Amber Room, all alone in front of the piles of food Minnifer had brought up, but I didn't feel sorry for her at all.

"Tell me more about my mother," I murmured when we'd cleared away the dishes and were sitting by the fire again, plates of apricot tart on our knees. "Tell me what she was like."

"Oh, she was lovely," said Minnifer dreamily. "And awfully powerful. She once conquered an entire army of weeshts who had found their way into the lands of living through an outhouse. And she did it with only her silver scissors and a rosemary lure! If you didn't know her, she might've seemed very grim and serious, but if you did . . . well, she couldn't have done enough for you. She was ever so generous, Georgina Brydgeborn was, and she cared about everyone, every person she met, and every ghost . . . and every orphan too."

"Was she the one who brought you here from the orphanage?" I was relieved to hear my mother was lovely, not like Magdeboor or Mrs. Cantanker. I hoped someone would speak of me that way one day, that perhaps I had inherited some of my mother's loveliness.

Minnifer nodded. "I still remember the day she arrived. She came in a great black coach, splendid and tall in her black cloak and shiny shoes, and it was all the orphan mistress could do to keep her from taking every one of the children back to the castle. Georgina couldn't bear to leave the others, you see, in that gray old house, with all of them pressed up against the windows, watching us rumble away to good food and warm fires. For every month after that, the orphanage got a chest of delicacies, and thick blankets, and dozens and dozens of new coats every winter. That was Georgina Brydgeborn for you, always trying to help everyone at once. . . . But I suppose being good is no guarantee that life will be good back. She worked all those years banishing troublesome spirits and making sure the lands of the living were safe. And it went to pieces before her eyes."

"Because of me?" I asked. "Because I was kidnapped?"

"Not *just* because of you," said Minnifer kindly. "Things have been going downhill for witches for ages. Maybe the other families wouldn't say so, but it's true. They've become like violins in museums, or toys on high shelves. Quite useless. They don't remember how to fight the dead. And yet the dead are still out there, perhaps closer than ever."

I remembered Mr. Grenouille's words in the morning room as the light spilled in between the drapes: "Whatever came for you all those years ago, whatever killed your family, may well still be lurking nearby."

"Have either of you ever heard of someone called the

Butcher of Beydun?" I asked, picking at the crust of my apricot tart.

"Heard of him?" said Minnifer. "Everyone's heard of him, though we all hope we'll never *meet* him. He's the king of a city deep in the fogs of the underworld, a city of ash and cinders, all black and burning and full of lost souls. He's the one Magdeboor brought back with her from her travels. But he's long gone. He was banished when she was burned up in the north wing."

Long gone? I wondered. Only he's not. He was here ten years ago to take me away. And if he's found his way back, how far behind him is Magdeboor?

Later, after I had said good night to Bram and Minnifer and was crossing the great hall toward the stairs, I heard a sound from the front doors. They were standing open, framing the woods and the wild dusk and two figures on the steps, silhouetted against the pale branches in the garden.

One was most certainly Mrs. Cantanker. The other

was small and hunched. I pressed myself into the shadows of the dragon staircase, straining to hear what they were saying. All I caught was Mrs. Cantanker's low purr and the occasional coo from the stranger. And then Mrs. Cantanker turned, and I saw she was holding a candle over a little wheelbarrow, or perhaps a wagon. It was heaped with treasures: pictures in gilt frames, silver saucers, and a long fur-lined dressing gown stitched with hibiscus flowers.

Mrs. Cantanker handed the wagon over, and I saw the second figure clearly for a moment—a pale, sharp-faced little man in riding boots and black coattails cloven like the hoof of a goat. He bowed to Mrs. Cantanker and doffed his hat. Then he bumped the wheelbarrow down the steps and creaked away toward the woods, whistling a jaunty, slightly grating little tune.

Mrs. Cantanker returned inside and closed the doors, looking back over her shoulder as she slid home the bolt. She passed within three feet of my hiding place, her expression stony. The light of her candle danced across the elegant bones of her face and winked in the jewels at her throat and on her fingers, particularly on a blue ring with a tiny spider etched into its depths. She did not see me, watching from the shadows.

Chapter Nine

BY my third week in Blackbird Castle, I was beginning to wonder whether Vikers's arrival, and the fact that I could see spirits from beyond the veil, had simply been bouts of extraordinary good luck.

"You're the worst witch I've ever met," Mrs. Cantanker told me one afternoon, as I tried desperately to reverse a spell I'd cast. It had come out wrong, and instead of all the toads in the pond becoming my friends and doing my bidding, they had gone to war with one another, charging in glistening green battalions across the lawn, their croaks echoing up to the tower tops. "How will you get ghosts to follow you into the underworld if you can't even get *toads* to follow you around a muddy puddle?"

She waited, as if expecting a reply, but there was none, and she knew it, and so I stood there forlornly, avoiding her gaze. At last I mumbled something about how I'd get it right next time.

"Next time . . . ," Mrs. Cantanker sniffed. "There is no next time for a witch. What do you suppose an attacking moorwhistler will do if you tell it you'll get it right next time? It will eat you, that's what! No, Zita, you are either capable, or you are not, and I'm beginning to think you're incapable of anything except stumbling about looking belligerent."

I stared at her, a bit stunned. Then the little flame kindled in my belly, and I was angry.

I am capable, I thought. I was sure I could do every task she gave me if only she would stop calling me quite so many names. She could go from whispers to rage within seconds, and when she raged I became flustered, and when I became flustered, I made mistakes, which made her rage more, which in the end left us both quite exhausted. But I was determined to improve. If I became a great Blackbird, I could break the ephinadym mulsion curse. I could try to bring my mother and adopted siblings back from the dead. And then I could throw Mrs. Cantanker out on her ear.

She was hatching something, I was sure of it. The League of the Blue Spider . . . that was what the marble prince had told me to investigate, and it could not be a coincidence that Mrs. Cantanker had a ring with a blue spider in it on her littlest finger. But what was the league? I wished I could be finding out instead of herding toads and being screamed at.

I'd been kept perpetually busy the last few days. Herbology in the morning, zoology in the afternoon, and sometimes, if Mrs. Cantanker was feeling particularly energetic, crypt visits after sunset. She would rap on my door and drag me out to the graveyard, where we would open a stone sarcophagus and descend the stairs to speak to the skeletons and ghosts who lived below. She would have me listen to their stories and write them down in my notebook, and though these tales were doubtless interesting to the wakeful, they were awfully tedious to someone longing to be tucked into a warm bed.

I often felt I wasn't learning any of the things I was supposed to. And I was given no opportunity to learn them on my own. Whenever I was in the High Blackbird's study, Mrs. Cantanker made sure I did not touch any of the books but the ones she gave me, and as for the Library of Souls and any other rooms where books of a magical nature could be found, she kept them firmly under lock and key. "What are you hiding from me?" I wanted to ask her. "What sort of teacher does not want her student to know things?"

It was several days after the incident with the toads when something happened whose importance I would not understand until many months later. I was balanced on a marble bench in the frosty gardens, a book on my head, waving my arms foolishly. My back was to the woods,

my face to the castle. Mrs. Cantanker paced about, shouting orders at me, her skirts rustling through the flaming
leaves. She called this exercise "the language of clouds,"
and the idea was that if you listened very closely and said
the proper words you could divert the weather, speed its
arrival if you required thunder, rain, and lightning, or
send it in another direction entirely if you wanted sun.
Personally, I thought it best to leave the clouds to do as
they pleased, but when I told Mrs. Cantanker this she
said, "Personally, I think it best if you keep your thoughts
inside your head where they will not bother me. Now do
as you're told."

I made a face at her when her back was turned and
resumed my flailings. I hadn't yet confronted Mrs.
Cantanker about her thievery. I felt like I ought to, that
it would be a small sort of revenge for all her meanness.
But what would I say? And what would she *do* if she knew
I had spied on her? The thought of her selling away my
family's things made me furious, and yet the real question was *why*. Why steal our treasures when she was

already so rich? And who was the little man in the coat like a cloven hoof? There had been something not right about him, something strange, and there was something not right about Mrs. Cantanker too. I wasn't quite at the point where I believed she might have had a hand in the murdering of my family, but it *had* crossed my mind.

My arms began to ache. The book on my head—"It will aid your poise and posture," Mrs. Cantanker had informed me—wobbled dangerously. From the wizened branch of a nearby elm, Vikers watched me, a glint of amusement in his eye. I scowled at him, but he only ruffled his feathers and settled onto the branch so comfortably I wanted to scream.

As for the clouds, they ignored me. There were quite a lot of them, puffy and billowy and very far away, but they didn't seem at all interested in my efforts to commune with them. The sun was shining brightly, melting the frost. . . . My eyes traveled along the toothy contours of the castle, up its spires, to the forest of chimneys sprouting from its many-angled scalp. Rows upon rows of windows stared blankly back, milky eyes reflecting the trees and the sky—

"Concentrate!" Mrs. Cantanker barked. "The clouds are practically standing still. Have you decided to slow them down?"

I haven't decided anything, I thought, but I said, "Yes," just so she'd leave me alone.

High up near the roof, I spotted a window quite unlike the others. It was shaped like a diamond resting on its tip. And all at once, I realized there was a face looking out of it—a pretty heart-shaped face, golden curls flashing. Then the clouds were rolling and breaking overhead and the window was a mirror, showing only the busy sky and the sunlight.

I fell from my bench with a gasp. The book went bouncing into a thicket. And it began to rain.

"Well, well," said Mrs. Cantanker, opening a pointed black umbrella. "A success at last!"

She did not offer any shelter to me. Instead she led me into the woods, which were quickly becoming just as wet and miserable as the gardens, and insisted on taking me to the grave of an ancient Blackbird named Pater Ribbons and introducing me to his almost catatonic ghost. I stood in my soggy stockings, scribbling away in my notebook and hoping to die, or at least to faint.

Whoever came for my family won't even need to curse me if things continue like this, I thought. *I shall freeze into a statue naturally.*

I returned to my room, bedraggled and dripping, and fell face-first onto my bed. Vikers stood guard atop the headboard, watching the door with sharp little eyes.

"Vikers?" I mumbled into my pillow. "I'm not sure I'm cut out to be a witch."

Vikers let out a disinterested caw, as if to say, "I'm not sure I'm cut out to be a crow. I've always felt I should be a well-pruned topiary. Yet here we are."

I felt my clothes beginning to soak the sheets and forced myself to get up, peeling myself out of my witch's uniform and slipping into one of Greta's fine nightgowns.

Then I stuffed my feet into fluffy slippers and scurried to the fireplace.

I ought to be out investigating the castle, but I was damp and miserable, and all I wanted was a fire and a mug of tea. Why was it always so cold in this house? I spotted a stack of wood by the hearth and a full coal scuttle, and set to work laying out the coal and lighting the kindling with the flint box. It began to burn fitfully, and I had just settled myself in front of it when I noticed that none of the smoke was going up the chimney. Instead it churned out of the fireplace, filling the room. I coughed and ran to the windows, throwing the casements wide.

"Well done, Zita," I muttered, as freezing air poured in.

I went back to the hearth and brushed up the little fire, throwing it into the ash bin. Then I got on hands and knees and peered up the chimney, feeling for the blockage. I braced myself for the worst, remembering the poor sparrows in Mrs. Boliver's chimney. But this time there was no nest or charred little bodies. There was a book, perched on a ledge and almost completely blocking the shaft.

I pulled it down and wriggled out of the fireplace, brushing the soot from my knees. The book was small and plain and had certainly seen better days. Its cover was scarred leather, and when I opened it, most of the pages fell out in a cascade of ash. It must have been in the chimney for some time, the thick cover never catching, only mottling, while the pages inside were eaten away. And then, somehow, it had fallen across the opening, alerting me to its presence.

"Vikers?" I said, and he flew over and landed on my shoulder. "What d'you suppose a book is doing in the chimney?"

I ran my fingers over the inside of the cover, admiring the once-lovely endpapers. They were the color of willowware, white and blue. Someone had written in a childish, unsteady hand:

Greta Brydgeborn, May 27, Year of the Twist-Horned Ram
Some of the pages were still intact, badly burned

around the edges but holding together. For a moment I was sure there were lines of writing on them—two eyes made of letters, periods, and question marks, which blinked at me. But when I looked closely, it was only specks of ash. It seemed as if the words had fled from my candlelight, pressing themselves to the edges of the paper.

I squinted, bringing the candelabra closer. Then I pulled the light away and the words crept out again, shyly, dancing like little figures across the page.

Greta . . .

Greta . . .

Greta, darling . . .

"I'm not Greta," I whispered.

But the book did not hear me.

Greta, where are you? Why have you left me in the dark? The other Blackbird is here. I feel her power, but it is still weak and unsteady. She needs her Anchor.

"The other Blackbird? Do you mean me?"

The words became sharp and angular.

Greta!

Are you listening?

Greta, you fool, do something!

Murder!

Murder!

MURDER! The Dark Queen moves in the shadows—

My heart wriggled into my throat. I slammed the book closed, but still it seemed to scream at me, the ink oozing in slimy tendrils across its charred cover.

She will kill the Blackbird hatchling. The three tasks will be completed, and then will come that pale friend, and all his beasts with him—

Greta . . .

Don't

let them

in—

I stuffed the book onto its ledge inside the chimney and scrambled back on all fours. The Dark Queen had to be Magdeboor. The pale friend was most likely the

Butcher of Beydun. As for the Blackbird hatchling they were going to kill, well . . . that was most definitely me.

That night I lay in my sea of feather beds, the lace like the froth of waves on the shore, the pillows like clouds scudding across the sky, and me floating in the center of it all, my arms outstretched, my eyes closed.

And then I heard a sound. It was coming from the door. I rolled onto my side, opening my eyes. No light shone across the threshold, and nor was there the smell of candle wax or kerosene that usually accompanied a nighttime wanderer. But *something* was out there, scratching gently at the wood.

I shivered. The room was icy cold. The drapes were open and the moon peered in like an enormous eye, its silvery tears drenching the floor and the bed things.

The scratching continued. Stealthily, I slipped from under the sheets and crept to the fireplace, lifting the poker. Then I padded to the door, pressing my ear to the wood. The scratching stopped.

"Who is it?" I whispered. "Who's there?"

Whoever it was did not see fit to answer me, so I gathered my courage and wrenched open the door, brandishing the poker ferociously. The corridor was empty. I glanced down it, then up at the ceiling, remembering what I had learned of ghosts and wishing I'd brought my sachet of herbs or my silver scissors with me. But the ceiling was empty too. . . . And then I felt a soft brush against my ankle, like a breath of cold air. On the ground was a dog—a small black pup, like a puff of coal smoke. It stood gazing up at me with solemn, mirror-bright eyes.

"Hello, little thing," I said. And then I swayed, the memory flashing once more through my mind.

A little girl in white, walking toward the woods. At her heel, a black pup, barking and whining. Something is waiting up ahead, just inside the shadows of the trees. The dog yaps desperately, but the girl keeps going. She is curious. She has always been curious and brave, and her hand is outstretched, for she does not yet know what fear is. She reaches the edge of the wood and looks up—

It was Teenzy! My dog! I was about to crouch down to comfort her—why was she peering at me so sadly?—when she turned, gazing into the dark. She let out a sharp warning bark, just as she had all those years ago. One bark, two, echoing down the corridor. I worried she might wake someone. I tried to scoop her up. But suddenly she was gone, my arms closing on empty air. I turned back to my room, Teenzy's bark still ringing in my ears. . . .

My blood ran cold. Standing face-to-face with me, her nose an inch from my own, was Greta. She was still encased in her dripping cocoon. Her eyes were open, unmoving. Then she blinked. I opened my mouth to scream.

Greta shuddered. Her stony mantle melted away, and she looked as I imagined she must have looked in life, all golden curls and sparkling eyes. She peered straight through me, as if I were the ghost and she were alive. And then she turned, and I saw the flash of a silver chain just below the hollow of her throat. Hanging from it was

a long key with an ivory handle, its tines in the shape of
a leaf.

"Greta?" I whispered. "Greta, what happened to you?"

She continued to stare straight ahead, swirling her
dress to and fro in the moonlight. Then Teenzy scurried
over the floorboards and Greta chased her, and they both
vanished into the wall behind an old threadbare tapestry.
I heard a musical little laugh. Then I was falling, down,
down, through rings of blackness. . . .

I sat up with a start. Frost. Frost on the bedcover, frost
on the walls, my breath forming clouds in the air. And
clutched to my chest, just under the comforter, was the
key with the ivory handle, its tines shaped like a leaf, its
metal cold as ice.

Chapter Ten

I'D never looked particularly closely at the tapestry before. It was ancient and threadbare, lined with frayed yellow silk. One side was stitched with bright colors, a gathering of fine ladies and gentlemen dancing. The other side had the exact same number of figures, only they were skeletons, and all was dim and dark. The skeletons were not dancing. They stood still as piers in an ocean, their heads turned, watching the revelry in the lands of the living. I couldn't tell if they were envious, sad, or angry, but it was clear that they were terribly interested in the dancing and brightness, and that the living were entirely oblivious to them.

I lifted the thick fabric, my fingers brushing over a panel, three tiny brass hinges, a keyhole. . . . Like a knife into butter, I slipped Greta's key into the lock. I felt the tines twisting, shivering. Then the panel swung smoothly inward and I was peering down a low stone passage, barely high enough for a child.

I whistled for Vikers. There was no answer. He must have flown off to conduct whatever secret business crows do at night. I wished Bram and Minnifer were here, even the marble prince, anything to break the silence of that yawning black opening. Of course I could have closed the panel and run back to bed. But I was a housemaid— nosiness was part of my essence. So, lighting my candelabra and brandishing it in front of me like a weapon, I made my way into the dark.

The passage was extraordinarily narrow. I pressed myself sideways, my feet shuffling through what sounded like leaves or paper. When I lowered the candelabra, I saw that the floor was entirely covered in letters, discarded toys, scrolls, and books. I went around a corner, then another, and then I ducked under a low-hanging lintel into a cozy little room. A leaded window shaped like a diamond resting on its tip looked onto the garden below. With a shiver I realized it was the one I had seen Greta peering out of, her pale face pressed to the glass.

My skin tingled. *Greta's secret room!* It was just as messy as her closet. I spotted glassy-eyed dolls, a life-sized painted rocking horse, a mountain of plush animals. Witchy things too—curious artifacts and treasures, little silver bells with mahogany handles, stacks of ancient coins, necklaces made of bones. Garlands of dusty ivy and laurel were draped along the shelves, and many candles, pink and lemon yellow, smelling of roses and citrus, dripped down their wrought-iron holders. In one corner there was a lamp hanging from a crooked wooden staff and a puffy armchair covered in violet upholstery.

But mostly there were books. This was a secret miniature version of my mother's library in the High Blackbird's study. Just as in hers, the shelves went all the way to the ceiling. There was even a ladder on a brass track, though I suspected it could hardly move in this mess. I picked my way around the room, fingers brushing over the gold-lettered spines.

Lunaline Mockshard's Advanced Spiritism

Banishment and Invocation, Book Seven

How to Travel the Roads of Death and Return Unscathed—A Practical Guide for Young Ladies and Gentlemen by Absinthia Klarmp

A bookstand stood in the center of the room, along with an inkwell and a quill. The book that was open on it was enormous, and when I lifted my candelabra I expected to find it full of symbols and mysterious magical references. But no . . .

The sparrow, when it saw that it was not welcome among the beautiful yet flightless peacocks, wheeled up into the sky, where it found a small castle nestled like a jewel in the clouds. . . .

I laughed in delight. It was a book of fairy tales!

I felt as if I had won the best prize at the Cricktown

fair. The key Greta had given me, the strange little book, and now my own secret chamber where I could retreat whenever the world or Mrs. Cantanker became too much to bear. I doubted Greta had led me here out of the goodness of her ghostly heart. Most likely she expected something in return. But the thought that even the spirits were helping me was a comforting one. And perhaps not just the spirits. "There are thirty-seven bedrooms to choose from," Minnifer had said the night I had arrived. "But we thought you'd like this one best."

Had they known about this hidden chamber? I rather thought they had, and I felt a surge of gratitude for my secret allies.

I walked through the little room, admiring Greta's treasures, her scribbly watercolors and souvenirs from faraway lands. And then there was Teenzy again, just for a moment, perched atop the bookstand. She was gone as soon as I blinked, but when I approached, I saw there was something tucked beneath the book, half hidden under its back cover—a piece of paper, small and tightly folded.

A Waking Spell was written across the top of it, and when I unfolded it, I found an old and hurriedly written recipe:

To be placed around the cursed one's feet:
A ring of rose petals and rosewater mist to attract
  the soul's return
3 branches of blackberry bush, clipped of their thorns
1 twig from the treskgilliam tree
1 silver scissors bequeathed to a witch
1 Anchor

A waking spell? I thought. *To wake up whom?* But of course I knew. To wake up Greta. To wake my mother and John Brydgeborn, and to free them from their curse. Greta and Teenzy had led me straight to the answer. The rosewater and blackberry branches would be no trouble to get, and I had the silver scissors already. I had no idea what a treskgilliam tree was, or an Anchor, but I knew I was quite capable of finding out. I refolded the spell, tucking it carefully into my nightgown pocket. Then, loading my arms with as many books as I could carry, I tottered back to bed.

It was very late by then, the grandmother clock on the wall clanging midnight, but I was far too excited to sleep. Everyone in this house—everyone but Mrs. Cantanker—seemed to be depending on me, and I was determined not to disappoint them. I curled up under my comforters, and in the dim glow of the candles, I began to read.

The lands beyond the veil—ah, how little we know of these places, though we speak of them often. Those who have traveled there and returned to tell of it describe death not as a gray waste, as it is often imagined, but rather as a vertical labyrinth of caverns and gardens, woods and marshes, huge teeming cities, transportation systems, the great river, waterfalls, and villages of lost souls. At the top are green pastures and soft light for the good, and at the bottom, descending deeper and deeper in hellish rings and circles, are darkness, smoke, and clanking machines for the wicked. Most souls arrive somewhere in the middle. Some very bad ones are cast straight down into the depths, where the green light and foliage of paradise are but a distant dream. . . .

The more I read, the more I began to realize Mrs. Cantanker was not a very good teacher. She was skirting vast swaths of history, telling me nothing about the heroic feats my family had performed, or of the high-ranking dead, or the names of the cities and geography of the underworld, or *anything* about breaking curses.

I moved from book to book, admiring the illustrations and doing my best to sort out the words.

Those in the darkest, most miserable depths of the spirit realm will always be striving to cross back into the lands of the living. They are drawn to its light and laughter like moths to lanterns. If they can escape their bonds, they wander, wailing, through the forests and villages of the dead, searching for a way to cross. Like wolves hunt rabbits, these warped spirits hunt for souls. And what better hunting ground than the lands of the living, where souls are bright and plentiful, and spatter the world like stars? Beware of deep caves and trees split by lightning, for that is where the dead crawl from. Beware of windows without curtains and lamps burning untended, for that is how they will find you, creeping closer, gathering in the shadows, wicked and hungry and so very cold. . . .

I shivered, glancing toward my own windows and thinking how inviting they must look from a distance: glowing pinpricks of light, no doubt, warm and cozy, the spirits out in those dark woods caught like fish in a net, watching and waiting for when they might become untangled. I stood and pulled the curtains shut, then dove quickly back into bed. Then I undid the clasps on a large old book bound in purple leather, and began to search for references to a treskgilliam tree and an Anchor.

There was nothing about the tree, not in the purple book nor in any of the encyclopediae but there were plenty of references to Anchors. It seemed to be one of the three elements essential to becoming a full-fledged Blackbird.

First was her initiation: Could she see the dead? If yes, then everything else could be taught. Second was her animal servant. Vikers was mine, and just then he was sleeping fitfully by my side, dreaming crowish dreams and muttering. The third was her Anchor. All the witches in Greta's romances and fairy tales seemed to have one, and it seemed to come in many forms—a Manzemirian chess piece, a bejeweled egg, a plain tallow candle, a black iris dried to a crinkle and pressed into a locket. The Anchor kept a witch from blowing away in great winds, or from being devoured by clouds of darkness, and in one story, it even seemed capable of reversing spells and bringing back souls from beyond the veil.

My eyelids began to droop, the sentences stretching and twisting and biting their own tails. I didn't have an Anchor, and Mrs. Cantanker had never so much as breathed a word about it. But that would have to change. Tomorrow the search would begin. I scratched Vikers's head, and settling into my nest of pillows and books and sweet-smelling paper, I fell asleep.

Chapter Eleven

EARLY the next morning, while the light was still a ghostly silver on the gardens and Pragast Wood was hazy with mist and frost, I rushed down to meet Minnifer. She was in the Hunting Room, scrubbing ferociously at the fireplace grate. I dropped down next to her, snatching a bristle brush from her bucket and setting to work as well. She looked at me as if I had just sprouted a second nose from my forehead, but I wasn't about to stand and jabber while she worked, so we scrubbed at the filthy hearth together, and I told her about the night before.

"You found the secret library?" Minnifer whispered when I had finished.

"So you *do* know about it." I rocked back on my heels, brushing the hair from my eyes. "I found a waking spell too. And Greta's book, though it wasn't a regular book. It wrote in itself, and it didn't seem to . . . well, it didn't seem to know Greta was dead."

"Poor thing," said Minnifer, as if the book had feelings of its own. "It was her book of all things, you know. She used to carry it everywhere with her."

"Did she? What's in a book of all things?"

"All things, of course!" said Minnifer, giggling, and then Bram came in wearing a belt of tools to adjust the gas lamps, and Minnifer jumped. "Oh, it's you," she said, but her face had gone pale, any trace of mirth draining from it. "Look, Zita, we're not allowed to talk about it, so don't ask, and don't try to make us. . . ."

"It was Greta's Anchor, wasn't it," I said, remembering what I had read the night before. *The other Blackbird is here. She needs her Anchor.* "Do you think . . . Do you think I have one?"

Both Bram and Minnifer went very still. When Minnifer spoke again, it was as if she were feeling her way across thin ice, as if each word might plunge her into freezing waters. "You could look for it," she said. "You could find it. Greta loved books, so that's what hers was, but yours could be anything. A little dagger, a figurine, a brooch—something you've got a sentimental attach-ment to, or something bequeathed to you by someone you loved. It's the most powerful of any witch's tools, that's what I heard, like a sort of lifeline. In the days when the Brydgeborns crossed over into the lands of the dead regularly, it's what kept them bound to home, to family and light and all that's good in the world. . . . But Zita?" Her voice became suddenly low and frightened. "Don't tell Mrs. Cantanker any of this. Please? She'll think *we* told you, and she'll . . . she'll . . ."

"She'll what?"

Minnifer said nothing, only clutched my fingers so hard I felt she might snap the bones. "Or something terrible will happen," Bram had said, the day in the corridor, and I had no doubt it was true.

"I promise," I said, pulling my hand away. "I won't let Mrs. Cantanker hurt you."

But I did not promise not to look for my Anchor, and I left the Hunting Room at a run.

Mrs. Cantanker was in a stormy mood when I arrived in the High Blackbird's study. She wore a lovely gown of gray silk trimmed with emerald ribbons, but the hem was soaked, and little half-moons of dirt peeked from under her fingernails. Her face was paler too, and she had a windblown look about her, as if she had just come in from a walk. *What* has *she been up to?* I wondered. *Rooting about in the woods?*

"Zita," she snapped. "Read the chapter on herbal remedies for frostbite in Ostermunden's *Garden,* and please don't speak to me. I don't think I could bear it."

I sat down with the book, my face expressionless. I didn't know if she was the one responsible for enchanting

Bram and Minnifer, and making them unable to tell me all they knew. She wasn't a witch, after all, and she *had* been my mother's friend, which must count for something. And yet Bram and Minnifer were clearly terrified of her. . . .

My lesson was an endless exercise in chopping herbs at precise forty-five-degree angles and making sachets to ward against low-level weeshts and churchyard boggles. I ruined my recipe three times and almost snipped off my finger, my mind busy with different problems. I was glad when Mrs. Cantanker complained of a headache and sent me away.

I went at once to the kitchens in search of Bram and Minnifer. They were gone, but there was a note dangling from one of the braids of garlic among the rafters, tied there with a blue ribbon.

For Z: We're down to the village for groceries. Be back in the afternoon. Please don't—

Here the note turned into a series of squiggles and dots, as if the writer had suddenly forgotten how to hold a pencil. The whole thing was signed:

B + M

Well, at least nothing bad had come from me asking too many questions about Anchors. I puttered about the kitchens, cutting myself slices of bread and cheese and eating them quickly. Then I whistled for Vikers, who had taken to responding to my calls almost at once, and together we set off through the castle in search of my Anchor. We journeyed through the formal rooms this time, and up the dragon stairs, which seemed to heave slightly under me, as if it were taking great, slow breaths. We pottered about in the sumptuous bedrooms that faced the front, the sitting rooms and dressing rooms. I ran my hands over everything, figurines to fire pokers, amphisbaena skins to zygadenes. I frightened household ghosts out of drawers and scolded with lavender the spirits who tried to frighten *me*. I opened wardrobes and put on hats, hoping one of them would make me into a real witch. None of it worked.

It was evening by the time I gave up. I was almost back to my room, intent on unloading my witch's equipment and going in search of dinner—a much more manageable quest—when I saw the blue stairs again. They weren't at all where I had seen them last. Now they stood at the end of a small landing, peeking from behind a carved mahogany pillar like some shy yet sinister creature. They seem to be calling to me, coaxing me toward them. But no sooner had I spotted them, than something even stranger happened. The castle seemed to close itself over them, a panel slamming across them. The blue staircase's dark recess was suddenly gone, and farther down the corridor, next to my room, another door creaked slowly open.

A warm glow shone out of it, cozy and orange, as if a fire had been lit inside the room, and as I crept closer I glimpsed that great tree again, its branches snaking across the ceiling, its roots coiling beneath the tiles, sending them up in humps or shattering them altogether.

I stepped in slowly, feeling as if I were in a dream. It was so quiet. A fire *had* been lit in the hearth, though there was no one there to enjoy it. And though the air was perfectly still, the tree's leaves rustled softly, whispering like a thousand pointy tongues, coaxing me in a much sweeter language than that of the blue stairs. I picked my way over the roots, marveling at such a huge tree being squashed into a such a small room. And all at once, I saw that there was a face in its trunk.

It seemed to have grown there naturally, and it almost looked like the face of an ancient man with brown and wrinkled skin, and a crackly green beard made of lichen. Its mouth was pressed into a crooked line, and its eyes were closed. *Could it be?*

"Are you . . . ?" I whispered. "Are you the treskgilliam tree?"

There was a slight sound—a tiny, tiny *creak*. The coals in the fireplace popped and shifted. Then the rustling of the leaves swelled, and a deep voice, like bark rasping against bark, said, "Treskgilliam? Is that what they are calling me these days?"

I gathered my thoughts, sure this was another of the castle's attempts to help me. Then I said, "I think it is. You see, sir, it's like this: my family has been cursed, and the castle we all live in is in trouble. You *do* know you live in a castle, don't you? Anyway, it's a very wicked, complicated curse, and I'm trying to break it with a waking spell, and the waking spell calls for a twig. One of your twigs, to be precise."

"A waking spell?" The tree let out a languorous creak, and all its many leaves shivered again, the sound so silvery and bright it made the hairs on my arms stand on end. "I heard of a waking spell once. Ah, yes. Six hundred years ago, when I was but a little sapling, high in the hills of Westval . . ."

It was all I could do not to sigh. I knew the tree's character at once. Mrs. Boliver had been this way, and so had the marble prince, and Pater Ribbons, and half the ghosts in Blackbird Castle. They liked to talk, that was the trouble, usually about themselves, and even the slightest provocation could lead to hours of winding tales, some thrilling, and some so dull and pointless they made you want to plug your ears.

"How interesting," I said under my breath, slipping the scissors from my belt and hiding them behind my back. I spotted a newly budded twig, fresh and green and easy to snip, and stole around the trunk where the tree could not see me. I raised the scissors to the twig . . . as interested as I was in having conversations with magical objects, and as used to the concept as I had recently become, I was also in rather a hurry.

"In rather a hurry, are you?" said the tree, and with a start, I realized its eyes had moved and were now wide open, gazing pointedly at my brandished scissors. They were sap-colored eyes, polished and smooth as amber, but they were not rheumy or sleepy. They were alarmingly keen and intelligent. "And I'm sorry my tales make you want to plug your ears. You know, you ought to listen when your elders speak. You just might learn something."

I gulped. Had the tree read my mind?

"I'm sorry," I said, tucking the scissors hastily behind my back. "I didn't mean to be rude."

The tree's gaze softened. "Do not be sorry, little bird. One is allowed some rudeness when one is very busy. I know what danger this castle is in. I know what creeps around its edges, testing with tireless fingers the wards placed upon the windows and the stones. And I know what darkness is already inside it, lurking at its very heart. I was told you would be arriving soon. You seek to perform a waking spell, hmm? The one with blackberry branches clipped of their thorns? Silver scissors and an Anchor? A good spell, that. And I see you are uniquely qualified to cast it. A girl like you, who has been to the places you've been . . ."

My heart thrilled at the tree's words, but then I remembered myself and said, "I've not been anywhere, sir. Just Cricktown and the orphanage."

The tree raised its mossy brows. "But you are mistaken! You have traveled far and wide, and seen many things. You have even gone to the lands of the dead."

I almost dropped my scissors. "The lands of the dead?"

"Oh, yes! Your mind does not remember, but your bones do—your skin and your veins and your heart. A body does not forget dying."

All at once, a root caught me around the ankle. Something sharp pricked my stocking, and a bright golden light flooded me. I was not afraid. But suddenly my muscles deserted me and I slumped, feeling myself slip away from my body and float up like a breath of air, out of that cozy little chamber and into an endless, velvet blackness. . . .

My hand is in someone else's, very cold, with long yellow nails. I am so tired. We are walking through a dark land, cinders heaped into drifts around us, ash falling like snow. Every few steps I see a black iron cage, half buried in the soot. Skeletal fingers reach from them, pincers and claws, and the tentacles of moorwhistlers and phantasms, grasping blindly for some trace of light or comfort. . . .

The image blurs and changes. I see us from afar, me in my white pinafore, glowing like a little lamp amid the shadows. I am hand in hand with the Butcher of Beydun. He leads me through desolate woods, ruined towns, ever closer to some glowing red light.

Again, the vision shifts: I am back in the lands of the living, standing on the doorstep of the orphanage. My white smock is sooty, my hair full of twigs. At the end of the lane, a wispy figure flickers away into the dusk. And now I am rising, up, up over the orphanage's chimneys, with a sound like flapping wings. Higher and higher I fly, until I can see the whole orphanage from above. The little girl is let inside. The door closes. . . .

Years pass, the flowers in the fields blooming and dying and blooming again. And then there is my mother, splendid in a wide-brimmed hat and black veil. She arrives in an onyx coach and knocks on the very same door through which I'd gone.

"A Brydgeborn?" I hear the nun's voice echoing up into my ears. "Of the Brydgeborn Blackbirds? Madam, we have no such child here. This is a place for the lost and unwanted, not the scion of a powerful family."

My mother goes away again, but others come, some of them with blue spider rings glinting on their fingers, or tiny spider-shaped patches stitched to their collars. They are all looking for me, but they don't find me. The nuns always turn them away. "A Brydgeborn here? What notions!"

And now I am zooming back toward the castle. I glimpse

myself standing in the glowing room, the tree's branches snaking around me, and I hear its wooden voice creaking. "*To wake anything, to break any curse, one must have seen both sides, the living and the dead. And you, my dear, have seen both. You are much more than you think you are. But beware, for those around you are much more than you think they are too.*"

I came to my senses with a start. The tree had let me go. The little room had gone quiet, all the pointy leaves fallen still. And in my hand was the twig, as new and green as spring.

Chapter Twelve

THE weeks stretched on, October dying in a fizzle of embers, and November dawning gray and chilly as rain-soaked washing. My lessons became intolerably boring. "Copy chapters five through seven of Hiram Ninnypin's *Simulacra*," Mrs. Cantanker would order, enthroned behind my mother's great desk. Then she would sip black tea and read her sinister little pamphlets, while I puffed out my cheeks and set to work, copying pages upon pages of a book I was sure had been written by a swarm of rats with ink on their feet.

Once my daily lessons ended, I continued the

search for my Anchor. Sometimes I brought Bram and Minnifer with me. We made a game of it, running up the many staircases of the castle, playing hide-and-seek or tag and only narrowly avoiding the odd cursed corridor, the sudden swamps that gurgled up between the floorboards, and rooms such as the Parlor of Psychosis, whose mirrored walls would show you a little girl who was not really there and who would lure you into an endless maze of silvered glass.

I spent my evenings in the kitchens, playing cards, snapping beans, or chattering with Minnifer and Bram while we mended Mrs. Cantanker's mountain of pillowcases. And every night I stayed up late in Greta's secret library, the wind slithering like a great cat against the window, Vikers diving at any triggle that dared poke its head out of a crack, and me wrapped in feather comforters, rose-scented candles flickering all around, reading of ancient myths and heroic deeds and searching for any reference at all to Anchors, and to a spell called ephinadym mulsion. It was all very fun and interesting, until I remembered I was going to die soon.

Almost none of the books told me anything helpful. I began to wonder if deadly curses were not a respectable topic to write about, and I also wondered how you were supposed to break them if you couldn't read about them in books. But one night, just as I was about to give up for the day and go to bed, I found a reference, a single entry in a battered black volume called *Sturmangel's Book of Forbidden Spells.*

"Ephinadym mulsion," I read, burrowing into my comforter.

A dreadful enchantment, deemed illegal by the Great Greenleaf Charter and henceforth used only by the most devious of dark witches. It is a gateway spell—which is to say, it requires the sacrificing of three souls to the lands of the dead in the interest of bringing another soul into the lands of the living, allowing it to pass back and forth freely. Last known use: Magdeboor III of the Westval Blackbirds performed the spell in order to bring one of the high-ranking dead to Westval, a king of the underworld with whom she had become befriended during her travels there.

My heart beat faster.

The curse is a tricky one to cast, and for legal reasons, the process will not be detailed here. Even more difficult, however, is breaking it—that is, reuniting the souls with their bodies— which can only be attempted by those who have walked both the lands of the living and the lands of the dead. Furthermore, the curse breaker must have a deep bond with the ones she wishes to rescue, and must care for them deeply, for no death nor dark magic can be reversed without love.

It was eleven o' clock on a Saturday morning, and I'd just collapsed onto my bed, dejected and confused from another fruitless wander through the castle, when something heavy landed on the pillow next to me. Vikers followed a moment later, nudging me gently with his beak. I rolled over and saw that he had fished Greta's book out of the chimney again.

"Do you want me to read more fateful proclamations about how doomed I am?" I asked, pushing myself up on my elbows. "Because I'd rather not, if it's all the same to you, not right before dinner—"

Vikers pecked at my hand, as if to say, "Your dinner is *not* the current priority," and I squeaked and said, "All *right*, goodness . . . ," and lifted the book, flipping to the unburned pages. Once again the words surfaced from the paper, little *t*'s and *i*'s bobbing up like driftwood. But this time the words they formed were random, confused.

> *Teeth*

River

> > *Thorns*

> *Beydun*

And then, clearly and decisively:

Greta? Greta? Has the other one found her Anchor?

"She hasn't," I said bitterly. "But I'll have you know she has blisters on both her feet from walking about looking for it, so she's certainly trying."

Vikers let out a low caw.

Walking about? the book wrote in looping, slightly befuddled script.

Blisters? You showed her your study, did you not? And you left it there for her, did you not, along with the waking spell?

So she's found it! She's found it and she's well on her way to preparing for the battle ahead!

The battle ahead? I glanced toward the tapestry. "But I only found the spell, not the Anchor! I'm not ready for any battles!"

Both Vikers and the book of all things were silent for a moment. Vikers eyed me sideways. Then, suddenly, the book snapped closed and open like a mouth, and a row of huge ink-splattered words appeared in the middle of the page:

WELL, GO LOOK FOR IT, YOU NUMPTY!!!

I gasped and leaped out of bed. Then, with Vikers on my shoulder, the book of all things under my arm, and a candle to light my way, I headed into the passage behind the tapestry.

You could at least tell me what *I'm looking for,* I thought angrily, glancing around the secret library. There were a thousand things in here, and any one of them might be a magical token capable of binding me to all that was good in the world. But at least I had only one room to search now instead of the hundreds in Blackbird Castle. "I suppose there's only one thing to do," I said, rolling up my sleeves.

First I threw out all the musty flowers, pulled down the garlands, collected the dried sprigs of lavender and yellow bull's-eye from the herbology cabinet, and trooped with them down the servants' staircase and into a desolate courtyard, where I threw them in a heap. Once the study had been utterly deflorested, I climbed the stepladder and swung around the perimeter of the chamber so that I could open the window and let in the bracing air.

Then I organized the many baubles and artifacts, and all the witch's tools, lining them up carefully. I lifted each one in turn, hoping for some rush of unearthly fire to kindle in my fingertips, but all I got was a splinter.

I didn't dare bother the book of all things again. Instead I collapsed on the floor to think. I glanced about the chamber, which was now organized and dusted to within an inch of its life. "No Anchor," I said to Vikers, who had alighted on my shoulder. "Nothing."

Vikers didn't answer, only perched very stiffly and severely, like a guard dog. He was watching a small hole in the ceiling. It looked much like the one in my bedroom, and the ones in the ceiling in the corridor that Bram had been stuffing. A faint cooing was threading out of it, along with a skitter of mortar. It was almost as if a tiny miner was digging about with an even tinier pickax.

I watched the hole, wondering what was up there. And then, all at once, I heard another sound and looked down to see a little lumpen figure peering around a cauldron. It was plump and powdery gray, like a mushroom, and its eyes were glossy black.

A triggle!

It wasn't frightened. It stepped out of the shadow of the cauldron, bobbing across the floor toward me. Then another one popped from behind a pile of books, and another scuttled down from the crack in the ceiling. They congregated, squeaking to one another in small, high voices.

Vikers flew up to the top rung of the ladder and began

to caw threateningly. But I didn't see what his trouble was. I thought the triggles looked rather adorable. I wanted to pick one up and squeeze its soft little arms and tickle its chin.

"Hello!" I said, scooting over the floor toward them. "What do you want?"

They froze and turned to look at me, a bit accusingly, as if I had interrupted them. Then one of them crept forward, its head slightly bowed, peeking up at me with its great black eyes.

"Oh, you *are* sweet," I said, crawling a little closer. "What are you, hmm? A ghost of some sort?"

The triggle gave a little mew. Behind it, the others tittered. I reached out with one finger, and it reached out its own arms, like a child asking to be held. I leaned down. Greta's skeleton key slipped from my collar, dangling in front of the triggle's face. And no sooner had it caught sight of the key than its eyes widened, and it snatched the key from around my neck, darting away over the floor and giggling wickedly.

"*Excuse* me!" I leaped to my feet. "Give that back!"

But the triggles only laughed and dispersed like beetles before a broom. They tossed the key to one another, flashing, just out of reach of my flailing hands. I charged after them, smacking one of them very hard. It was like hitting a dusty pillow with a broom: a puff of green spores exploded out of it, and it went hurtling through the air and into the drapes, which it slid down, landing in a heap on the floor and looking quite dead. A moment later, it hopped up again and darted away, cackling maniacally.

One of the other triggles yanked on the hem of my skirt. Then four of his compatriots shoved the armchair into the back of my knees and I collapsed into it. By the time I had recovered, the key was darting very fast toward the hole in the ceiling.

"Vikers!" I shouted "Don't let them get away!"

With two beats of his wings Vikers reached the hole, hovering in front of it menacingly. The triggle with the key took one look at him and turned with a shriek, running across the ceiling in the opposite direction. Vikers extended a talon, almost casually, and snagged the key's silver chain. The triggle kept running, not realizing it was going nowhere. Then, like a grouchy old fisherman, Vikers began reeling it in.

I dragged the stepladder over and started up it. The triggle holding the key shrieked ever more desperately, unwilling to let go of its treasure but unable to flee. Other triggles, popping from behind candles and books, shrieked too, in commiseration. And then I reached the ceiling and plucked the key from the triggle's grasp.

"No," I said sternly. "Bad triggle. This is *not* for you."

It hung its head, still standing upside down on the ceiling. The others began to mope and whine, sounding like nothing so much as a bunch of spoiled babies. As I climbed back down the ladder, they reached out their hands for the key, weeping piteously. But Vikers flapped his wings, herding them into a pack, and they silenced, eyeing his scythe-like beak mistrustfully.

I wondered how many other things they had stolen

from this room, how many other shiny objects they had scuttled off with . . .

And then it dawned on me: the triggles! The triggles had stolen my Anchor! Greta had led me to its hiding place, and her book had told me where it was, and perhaps the Anchor *had* been in the secret room. But what if it was the exact shade of shiny and glittering to make a triggle want to snatch it? Now the only question was— where did triggles take their stolen bounty?

I whistled for Vikers and set off to find Bram.

Chapter Thirteen

I found Bram in the kitchens, ferrying baskets of onions, sides of ham, and cones of sugar out of the pantry in preparation for dinner. "Oh dear," he said, before I'd even begun my story, which made me think I must look fairly frantic.

"Oh dear what?" Minnifer demanded, poking her head up from her mountain of pillowcases. She clambered out from among them, and they both hurried over, squinting at Vikers and me.

"It's the triggles," I said. "The triggles have my Anchor!"

"The triggles?" Minnifer whispered. "Are you sure?"

"Almost positive. I know where it was supposed to be, and it wasn't there, and I caught a whole passel of them rummaging about—"

"Little *wretches!*" exclaimed Minnifer and Bram at once, and then Minnifer said, "We've got to get it back," with such conviction I thought she might be about to don a helmet and take up a sword.

"Do you know where they hide the things they snatch?" I asked, my heart thumping. "I thought you would, Bram, since you're always after them, and I just hope they haven't put it somewhere unreachable like under the floorboards or—"

But Bram and Minnifer were already pulling me out of the kitchen and down a corridor, their work forgotten.

"They've got little troves all over the castle," said Bram. "Sometimes they like to move them about, especially if they feel they're being watched. But they've got one main spot."

"Amsel's Tower," said Minnifer. "North wing."

"The burned one?" I said, dashing along with them, Vikers clutching to my shoulder for dear life and letting out a squawk of indignation at all the excitement.

Bram nodded. "We'll go through the forest. It's safer than climbing through all that rubble. There's a place where Pragast Wood creeps right up to the edge of the castle, and that's where the tower is. Looks like a broken finger. I've cleared it out twice, but the triggles keep filling it up again. . . . Here, put this on."

We had entered a little room, green cloaks on pegs, heaps of baskets, and rows of high black boots on the floor. Bram stuffed one of the cloaks into my arms and began pulling on a pair of boots. Vikers flew up to the gas lamp and perched there, watching us.

"Mrs. Cantanker will have a fit if she sees us with you and not at our work," said Minnifer, pulling on her own boots. "But we'll take you to the crack in the wall, and we'll keep watch while you go into the tower, and if Mrs. Cantanker sees us we'll just pretend we were out mushroom picking."

I nodded, and we donned the green cloaks, took up baskets from the pile, and set off across the gardens for the perimeter of trees.

It was a lovely afternoon, bracing and sharp, the mountain air smelling of pine and stone and the coming winter. Vikers wheeled in the sky above. The last of the autumn leaves blew around us, and the sun took the edge off the cold and made my heart soar. The woods held no horror by day. Even the memory of my kidnapping seemed far off, as if it had happened to someone else, in a different forest, or in a dream.

"What a pretty place," I said, going to a tree and laying my hand against its trunk. I felt the sun-warmed bark under my fingertips, and beneath that, the thrum of some ancient power, the old, slow life of the tree itself.

"Yes," agreed Minnifer, but Bram frowned at us.

"It's not pretty," he said. "These woods are very old. Very odd. A place where the veil between the worlds has worn thin. There are loads of ghosts here."

"Well, I like it," I said, giving the tree a friendly pat.

"Anyway, it's the middle of the afternoon. I'm sure it's perfectly safe now."

"I don't think spirits tell time," Bram said, stomping across the moss and into the cool air beneath the trees. "It's all a hoax, what they say about midnight and the witching hour. Ghosts are either here or they're not. People just pay more attention in the dark."

Minnifer and I exchanged looks. Then we too stepped into Pragast Wood, picking our way among the mossy stones and fallen branches. Moths darted on the breeze, wings tipped in rust and amber. Mushrooms grew in the damp hollows, their spores collecting in dusty clouds that hovered over the ground. Sunlight barely penetrated the evergreen branches, but here and there, where there was an oak or an ash, and the leaves had fallen, it broke through in golden pools.

"What *are* they?" I asked. "The triggles. They look like what might grow on a wheel of cheese if you left it in the cellar too long."

"Maybe they do," said Minnifer. "No one really knows

where they come from. It's said they're what happens when a ghost stays in the lands of the living for too long, or that they're the spirits of the rich and greedy. But they've been spirits so long they're practically brainless. Mrs. Cantanker has somehow persuaded them to do little chores for her, but usually they just steal things."

"I suppose they hope they'll eventually have enough to pay passage into the spirit realm," I said, and Minnifer laughed.

"Well, they're never going to get there. As if the spirit realm wants triggles running about, stealing everything that shines! They're far too annoying."

We approached the graveyard and went through its crooked gate. Tombstones veiled in ivy pushed up around us like uneven teeth. Several mausoleums, grim little mansions black with age, lurked among the trees. I knelt to examine one of the tombs.

Miss Hyacinth Brydgeborn, it said. *Taken too soon at the age of 21 by a fangore in an unfortunate incident.*

Bram and Minnifer were already far ahead. I scratched at a bit of moss, trying to read about the unfortunate incident.

And then something on the ground caught my eye: a footprint, small and elegant—a lady's shoe with a heel.

Who had been out here? The footprint looked quite fresh. I parted the grass, saw another footprint, and another. The path led out of the graveyard, into a thicket of ancient trees. I scrambled to my feet and followed the track, pushing through another little gate and out beyond the edge of the graveyard.

There, deep in the creeping mist, was another mausoleum. It was larger than the others, dark pillars and a peaked roof, the doors shut tight. It looked proud, as if it did not care to be a part of the rabble in the graveyard anyway. The path wound toward it, ending at the foot of its cracked stone steps. I knew at once whose house this was: Magdeboor's.

The woods had gone silent. No sunlight fell here. The air was cold and heavy as a damp blanket. And then, for the briefest instant, I saw Greta. She was standing in the shadow of the mausoleum, in a thicket of brambles. Her dress was ragged, yellow silk and lace, torn and streaked with mold. Her gaze was ferocious, almost hateful. And in the blink that I glimpsed her, she lifted her hand to me, and I saw that her palm was scoured with a bloody brand—eight legs, a fat, round body. A spider.

I gasped, squeezing my eyes shut. When I opened them, Greta was gone, but I had not imagined her. The brambles where she had stood were coated in frost, and I still felt her gaze . . . an accusing glare, as if I had done something terribly wrong.

"Zita?" Minnifer was beside me, her voice loud in my ear. "Zita, what are you doing?"

I jumped. "Oh," I said, looking again at the mausoleum. "I don't know, I—"

But before I could say another word, Minnifer was pulling me back through the mist and into the graveyard, away from that brooding little house. "Stay on the path," she murmured. "There's no telling *what's* out there."

We came at last to the place where Pragast Wood crashed against the castle in a wave of oak and evergreen. Just as Minnifer and Bram had promised, there was an opening in the wall, and behind it an overgrown courtyard and the looming towers of the north wing.

"This is as far as we take you," said Minnifer, looking forlorn.

"If we're caught in there . . . ," Bram started to say. "Well, best not. Best not give anyone reason to think we're snooping."

I nodded. Then I whistled for Vikers, who flew down out of the sky to sit on my shoulder, and climbed over the mossy stones and into the courtyard.

Blackbird Castle's oldest wing was not at all like its inhabited ones. Charred battlements loomed against the blue sky like the fangs of some gigantic beast. The spines of rusting gates snagged at my cloak. Parts of the walls had collapsed, revealing the chambers behind them, like an opened-up dollhouse, and I saw grand drawing rooms, and little bedrooms higher up, all of them sleeping, frozen in time, tucked beneath shrouds of ivy. I glimpsed moldering paintings, tarnished silver on mantelpieces, a banquet hall blackened with cinders and overrun with vines, crystal and china still lying among the leaves. No thieves had come to relieve the Brydgeborns of these abandoned treasures. I supposed none had dared.

I crossed a stone bridge above a grassy, dried-out moat . . . and there was Amsel's Tower, beckoning to the sun like a crooked finger, as if hoping to lure it from its path across the sky. Vikers let out a long, foreboding caw.

"Shh," I said. "We don't want anyone to know we're here."

I gazed up at the tower, its missing roof and small gray windows. I imagined the triggles scampering through their little passageways, then out into the open and up that sheer stone face, vanishing into the arrow slits. *Little wretches indeed.*

I doubled my pace. At the base of the tower was a rotting door, and into this I inserted Greta's silver key, twisting it with all my strength. I might have been too enthusiastic, however, because the entire lock fell out with a clang, and the door yawned open without any sort of fight at all. I stepped into the dark mustiness of the tower.

All was quiet and still. I began climbing the winding stair, Vikers perched on my shoulder. The stair was made of wood, and I felt sure the whole construction would at any moment come away from the wall. Higher and higher I went, hopping over the holes where treads were missing, gulping down my fear when the staircase began to sway.

I was breathless and tingling all over with nerves by time I reached the top. The chamber was round and almost bare. Whatever furniture there had been lay piled up against one wall. And in the middle of the floorboards, glittering in the meager light, was a mountain of treasure absolutely swarming with triggles.

They climbed over the goblets and brooches like ants, cooing to one another and polishing the trinkets with curtain tassels and bits of rags. For a good long moment, they were too absorbed in their work to notice me standing there, gaping at them. Then Vikers made a small noise in his chest and they all froze, their faces tiny masks of alarm.

I froze too. There were quite a lot of them, and I wasn't sure I could fend them all off if they decided to attack. But then I realized I was alarmed by what amounted to a passel of sentient mushrooms, and I strode toward them, my cloak flapping behind me.

"I just want my Anchor back," I said firmly. "Just one thing, and you can keep the rest for all I care."

But the triggles did not seem willing to part with so much as a single coin. They slid down the pile and formed a ring around it, shouting in shrill voices. Their shrieking continued to rise, thinning into a single thread-like whine. And then one particularly bulbous one with a red-and-white toadstool head began to advance.

I looked at Vikers. Vikers looked at me. Then Vikers flew at the triggles, and they ran screaming up the walls, gathering on the ceiling like a wobbly, resentful spot of mold.

"One thing," I said again, peering up at all those wide black eyes.

I knelt before the pile. There were candlesticks and

silver platters, golden teaspoons and ruby necklaces, crystal toads, sapphire-eyed unicorns, and entire rolls of jeweled damask. But I knew my Anchor was here, under it all. I could feel it, a delicate pull at the edges of my mind. I began to lay out the treasures, piece by piece, until the entire floor was full of objects. Then, when there was only a heap of coins and little trinkets left, I pushed my arm into it, all the way up to my shoulder. I rummaged about, squinted, stuck my tongue out between my teeth. . . .

I felt it at once, a light sting of electricity against my fingertips. And then warmth, like the loveliest handshake from a friend. I withdrew my arm, a foolish grin on my face. Clutched in my fingers was a plain silver locket. It was oval, decorated only with a few ivy leaves. Etched into its cover in tiny, tiny writing were these lines:

For Zita Brydgeborn, last of her name. May this light always guide you home.

The words made my heart hurt. My parents must have chosen them, not knowing that everything was about to change, that they would never give the locket to me, that I was about to vanish and they would spend their remaining years searching for me in vain.

My fingernail found the locket's release and I clicked it open. Inside was a small pane of glass, and behind it was the morning room. But not a picture of the morning room. No, as I turned the locket to and fro, the room turned too, as if I were looking at it through a telescope. I saw the painted silk scrolls, the gilt chairs, and potted ferns. And then I turned all the way around and found myself suddenly face-to-face with three figures: Mother and Father and a baby who I suspected was me.

I'd never seen a picture of myself as a child. Mirrors had been forbidden at the orphanage for fear they would turn the children vain, and Mrs. Boliver had never hung up any, either, as she'd held the odd belief that they made her older with every passing day. For most of my life, I'd satisfied my curiosity with looking into pots and puddles, and trying to piece myself together out of the things others said I was and what I felt to be true. It was a bit of a shock, then, to see myself in the flesh. There was my wild hair and pinched face, and I had been dressed up until I looked like a rather turnip-y little root in a bonnet. We were sitting in front of a crackling fire. Papa had his arm around Mother's shoulder, I sat in her lap, and Teenzy was curled into a ball on top of a tasseled cushion, and we were all beaming at each other, as if we'd never been more delighted in our lives. And then my mother looked up, peering out of the glass, and I could swear she was smiling right at me, her face crinkling, bright and warm.

"Mother?" I whispered, leaning over the locket. "Mother, do you see me?"

But the image only sputtered and began again, like a loop, repeating itself over and over. I sat on the floor for some time, watching those smiling faces. Vikers rubbed his head against my cheek. Even the triggles went quiet, creeping down off the ceiling to stare at me with great solemn eyes.

After what felt like hours, I noticed the sunlight creeping down the wall and remembered Bram and Minnifer out in the woods. I got to my feet, clutching the locket to my chest. Then I nodded to the room, a nod of thanks. "Greta," I said. "I'm sorry for what happened to you, but I'm going to fix it."

I left the tower at a run, making my way crashingly down the stairs. The locket joined the skeleton key around my neck. Vikers wheeled above me in the gathering dusk. As I made my way across the bridge, I thought I saw Greta again, far back among the ivy, glaring at me. But before I could really tell, a billow of leaves blew up from the moat and she was gone.

Chapter Fourteen

I must have spent more time in Amsel's Tower than I'd thought, because Bram and Minnifer were not waiting for me at the gap in the wall. I found them half an hour later in the Room of Marble Heads, their green cloaks disposed of, rags and buckets in hand, diligently polishing the hundreds of ancestral busts. The busts were all whispering in stony voices, centuries of memories, gossip, and counter-gossip bubbling up out of their throats, and Bram and Minnifer were doing their best to look demure and busy. I saw why at once: Mrs. Cantanker was in the room next door, swirling about in flowered silks and filling a padded box with porcelain tea things.

Bram placed a finger to his lips. Minnifer winked at me. As soon as Mrs. Cantanker had retreated down the passageway, they rushed over.

"You found it?" Minnifer whispered, and she seemed far more excited than seemed entirely reasonable. "Was it where we said it would be?"

I nodded, pulling the glimmering locket from my collar. "And look what's inside."

I opened the clasp. There was the pretty room, the crackling fire . . . and there was my family, moving about and smiling. "Aren't they lovely?" I whispered.

Both Bram and Minnifer smiled too. "Yes," said Minnifer softly. "They *are* lovely. Now everything will be easier. You'll see."

Minnifer was right. Everything *was* easier after I found the locket. I didn't even notice Mrs. Cantanker's moods or rages, and because I didn't notice them, she seemed to give up having them quite so often. We trained with lures and coins and weapons in the Hunting Room, discussed the flora and fauna of the underworld, dissected an undead beetle. . . . Mrs. Cantanker even praised me on my lunges once, while I fought a straw mannequin with my silver scissors. I wondered if the change lay with me or with her, but I rather suspected it lay with me. Ever since I'd found my Anchor, I felt as if nothing could bother me. A lightness and a warmth seeped from the locket, and with it lying against my heart I felt nigh unstoppable. If the Butcher of Beydun was on his way, and the Dark Queen with him, he would not find *me* a half-fledged witch.

I had the treskgilliam tree's twig, my silver scissors, and the locket . . . now I had only to wake my family.

That night, after Mrs. Cantanker's lessons, I crept down to the dining room, my arms full of blackberry branches, and unlocked the gilt doors with my skeleton key. Then, using my locket for a light, I crept forward into the dark. The cocooned shapes lurked in the shadows ahead, that strange stone dripping from their collars and down their cheeks. As I approached, I heard a faint tickling, skittering sound, and for a terrifying moment I wondered if they were stirring, like creatures about to hatch. But no . . . with a shudder, I saw it was the food that stirred, slowly decomposing beneath a glistening sheen of maggots, roaches, and ants.

I was not afraid of insects, not in the least. I *was* afraid of the still, soundless shapes in the chairs, but I told myself I mustn't be. They were my family. I loved them, didn't I? Or at least, I loved their souls, which were very far away now. Gathering every scrap of courage I possessed, I sat myself on the floor crosslegged, next to my mother's chair, and peered up at her. She looked different than she did in the locket. I wasn't quite sure why. I supposed that was what death did to people, emptied them of all they really were.

You'll save us, won't you, Mother? You'll come back and make all this right.

Something twinged in my heart, quivering like a plucked string. I wanted so badly to wake her. I wanted the cocoon to melt away, the lights to blaze in the chandelier, and the castle to fill once more with people and laughter. I wished for it so much it hurt. And then, when I was done wishing, I set to work.

First I dragged all three chairs away from the table and pushed them back-to-back. Then I laid out the silver scissors and the green twig from the treskgilliam tree on the floorboards, and set to clipping the thorns off the blackberry branches, every last one, my eyes straining in the dimness. I slipped the locket from around my neck and draped its chain in an arc, the clasp open, light shining from the glass pane. Last of all, I strewed the petals in a circle before spraying everything with puffs of rose water from my bottle.

I stood back to examine my handiwork. It looked perfect. It *was* perfect. In just a few moments I would no longer be alone in this castle, no longer the last of my line on whom everything depended. In just a few moments, the veil would part for a moment, and Mother and Greta and John would step through it, and I would no longer be an orphan.

"Wake up, Mother," I whispered. "Wake up, Greta, wake up, John Brydgeborn."

I closed my eyes, my hands clenched into fists. I thought I heard a sound—a rustling very close by. My eyes sprang open. A mouse was looking at me curiously through the ribs of the ham. It cocked its head, bright eyes glinting. But none of the figures had moved. I clenched my fists again, hoping and wishing and trying to feel all the love in the world, squeezing it from my heart like water from a rag.

Nothing. They did not wake up. The mouse grew bored and returned to its feasting.

In the end, I gathered up my scissors and the blackberry branches, put the treskgilliam twig back into my belt, and went to fetch a broom. I worked until deep into the night, pulling down the cobwebs and pushing about heaps of dust like snow. I worked until my hair stuck to my forehead and my arms ached, until I was too tired to cry.

I was only a housemaid, after all, and in those miserable hours, I was sure it was all I would ever be.

Chapter Fifteen

IT was well past midnight by the time I crept back to my room, shame and hurt filling my chest to bursting. I lay on my bed, curling into a ball atop the comforters and waiting for sleep to come. Vikers nudged my head with his beak and made soft burbling sounds, gentle as a dove. I kept my eyes firmly shut and tried to pretend it wasn't helping, but it was, and I was glad for the crow, glad for his kindness, though I'd not dared ask for it and was not sure I deserved it.

"I don't know what to do," I said to Minnifer the next morning. We were on the dragon stairs, she dusting the banister and I on the bottom step, slumped against the bejeweled newel post. My hair was coming out of its braid, my uniform was crinkled, and there were dark rings under my eyes from lack of sleep. Vikers sat on the dragon's head, his own head twisted down so he could stare into one of its ruby eyes. "I don't know what I did wrong. I got everything I needed to bring them back, and clipped every last thorn off the blackberry branches, and did everything just the way the spell told me. But they didn't come back."

Minnifer was looking over the spell, one hand swinging the feather duster, the other clutching the slip of paper. Every few seconds she cast me a worried glance. At last she said, "Oh dear," very quietly, and came down the stairs to sit next to me. She handed me back the paper, carefully refolded into a tight square. "Don't despair, Zita. I'm sure it wasn't useless. You wouldn't have gotten a powerful old spell for no reason, would you? It's bound to work for *something*."

But I didn't want it to work for anything else. I wanted my family back.

"I met a ghost during one of my lessons," I said after a while, staring across the checkerboard tiles of the grand hall. "She told me she was part of a great big web. And the other day I talked to the treskgilliam tree—you know, the one in the room next to mine?— and it showed me people going to the orphanage where I used to live, people with the sign of the blue spider on their fingers, or stitched into their jackets. Mrs. Cantanker has got one of those rings. I think the League of the Blue Spider is the web. I think all of them—Mrs. Cantanker included—are trying to bring Magdeboor back. And I think we're all stuck right in the middle, with no one to help us."

Minnifer slipped her arm around my shoulder. "We'll help each other, though," she said. "We'll find a way."

I allowed myself to wallow in self-pity for several more minutes. Then I gathered my cloak around me and stood.

"I don't know why Greta left me that spell," I said. "But whatever's coming, whatever killed my family, it's up to us to stop it. And I think the first thing we're going to have to do is get rid of Mrs. Cantanker."

This was easier said than done, however, for not fifteen minutes later I began to wonder whether Mrs. Cantanker might be planning to get rid of us first.

"You will have a test today," Mrs. Cantanker announced, as I clumped into the High Blackbird's study. She was not dressed in one of her usual gowns. Instead she wore handsomely cut trousers and an emerald green waistcoat, a lace bow at her throat and long black gloves that reached to her elbows. "I hope you're *well* rested."

I looked at her sharply. Was I imagining the malice in her tone, the amused quirk of her smile? With a pang of fright, I wondered suddenly if she knew everything, all the schemes I'd been hatching and the quests I'd been on these past weeks. I mumbled something agreeable and followed her through the corridors, my heart beating very fast.

We arrived in a large, desolate training hall. Once, it might have been a lively place, full of students practicing their lunges, entire rows of Blackbird siblings in dark cloaks and tool belts. But now it was miserable, pigeon droppings speckling the beautiful paintings and bits of straw drifting down in the warm morning sunlight.

"We've practiced long enough," said Mrs. Cantanker, leading me to a small writing desk against one wall. It had been laid out with various weapons and sachets of herbs. "Now we will see what you have learned. This is an important test—*vital*, in fact—so I expect you to do your very best."

She helped me equip my belt with star root, wormwood, rosemary, and honeysuckle. Then she positioned me in the center of the hall, and the test began.

"Most witches have very little offensive power," she said, circling me slowly while I stood in a shaft of light from a high window, my ears pricked, a silver coin in one hand, a rosemary lure in the other. "Our powers are slow, patient things: coins, trees, wind and rain, little nubs of roses in a pillow to ease a passing, and salt to guard against unlawful entry. But sometimes, more drastic measures are required."

The light lanced down around her. Her high-heeled shoes clicked on the gleaming parquet. I noticed she was holding an oblong box under one arm, lacquered red and inlaid with all the stages of the moon in mother-of-pearl.

"Wicked things grow in the lands of the dead," she said. "And sometimes they go where they're not sup-posed to. Sometimes they slip their borders, creep up on you unawares."

She was smiling at me oddly, and in that moment I could have sworn she could look right into my skull and see all the scheming, swirling thoughts inside. "No sweet bribes will be enough, then, no soft words or con-solations. No . . . All that is left for you is to strike! To wound!"

"What sorts of wicked things are you talking about, in particular?" I asked, my skin tingling.

"You'll see," she said, and opened the lacquered box, placing it in the center of the floor. Then she sniffed whatever lay inside, wrinkled her nose, and stalked away.

Nothing emerged, no ghost or djinn or cackling chicken-footed demon. I approached the box cautiously, peering inside. It was empty but for a small reddish-brown lump, like a large chestnut, lying in one corner. A sharp smell rose from it, rich and exotic, like the ancient bottle of jasmine perfume Mrs. Bolivar had kept under her bed. And in that smell, barely disguised, I caught the tang of cured meat. I could not decide if the smell was lovely or hideous, but it certainly caught one's attention.

"Pick it up," ordered Mrs. Cantanker, and I gulped. Knowing her, this would not end well, but I did as I was told. The lump was smooth, rather warm. From somewhere—close or far away, I could not tell—I heard a sudden barrage of whispers, high shrieks, and laughter. They coalesced into a long, low growl. Then, at the far end of the gallery, something heavy struck the double doors and they bowed inward.

I spun. "What was that?" I asked. "What's out there?"

The whispers and growls grew louder, as if an entire horde was pressed to the other side of the doors. Mrs. Cantanker's smile stretched. . . .

The creature exploded into the room—six-legged, oak leaves for a pelt, red sinew and snapping teeth and muscles that seemed to be made of thick vines. Its head was shaped like a spade, an enormous horn at its front. Its beady little eyes were fixed on me.

"An Elysian fangore!" Mrs Cantanker announced with a flourish, as if she were a circus master displaying her newest attraction. "And in your hand, the desiccated heart of a mandrake. It acts the way the color red acts on a bull, driving the beast to wrath. The smell is all over your fingers now, so don't even bother trying to run away. It'll only chase you, and you'll have the whole house in shambles."

I dropped the lump, wiping my hand desperately

on my dress. But it was too late. The monster hurtled toward me, its claws scrabbling for purchase on the floor. With a start, I saw there were human faces embedded in its belly, pale and gasping, milky eyes peering out from among the leaves and vines.

I screamed. On my shoulder, Vikers screamed too. The fangore let out a roar that set the windowpanes to rattling. And Mrs. Cantanker sprinted to a pretty gilt chair and sat down, watching me and the monster expectantly.

"*This* is my test?" I shrieked, diving out of the monster's path. "You know, usually students aren't supposed to be *eaten alive by their exams.*"

"Oh, don't be a baby!" Mrs. Cantanker shouted back. "Your mother conquered a fangore on her very first day as an underwitch, when it broke into the girls' dormitory. It's *quite* within your grasp!"

But I was not my mother, and I did not feel it was in my grasp at all.

The beast skidded to the end of the gallery, paused

a moment as if startled to find a wall there, and then charged back toward me. Lashes of what looked like filthy water flew from its hide with each swing of its great body. And yet all of the filth and refuse melted away the instant it struck the parquet.

Was the beast even real?

Perhaps it was some sort of illusion, a trick, the way Mrs. Cantanker's first test had been. Or perhaps it was a ghost and would simply pass through me on a breath of freezing air. I planted my feet, raised my hand.

The monster picked up speed, galloping toward me.

It's not real, I told myself. *It's not real, it's not real, it's not real—*

And then it caught me sideways with its great horn and swung me up into the air, and I landed with a crash on the parquet.

"Oh," I mumbled, rolling onto my back. "It *is* real."

"Use your scissors!" Mrs. Cantanker shouted. "For heaven's sake, fight!"

I pulled myself dizzily to my feet. My silver scissors

had fallen some ways off. The rosemary was still in my hand, but it looked as if it had shriveled up in terror. The fangore turned, eyeing me down the length of the room. It began to approach again, its many faces screaming and yowling. Vikers flew at it, attacking with beak and talon. The fangore merely extended one leg and punted Vikers away, sending him whirling into a large brass pot.

"Vikers!" I shouted. A reassuring squawk echoed from inside the pot, a squawk I was sure meant "I'm all right, but I think I'm going to stay here for the time being, thank you very much."

I didn't blame the crow one bit. The beast picked up speed, its claws glancing off the polished floor. I wished I could climb into a large brass pot as well. And at the last possible moment, I dove out of the fangore's way, skidding along the floor. The scent of brimstone and burning, damp graves and moss, washed over me, almost making me gag. The beast whirled, its gaze furious.

"Aye, little witch, with your lungs full of air,

"Shall we pop them like balloons, make your breathing quite rare?"

I began dragging myself toward my fallen scissors. I was almost convinced Mrs. Cantanker did not want me to survive this encounter. Perhaps some spying ghost or marble head had told her of my expeditions with Bram and Minnifer, or how I'd watched as she'd handed over Brydgeborn treasures to the little man in the cloven coat. Perhaps whatever purpose she had been keeping me for had entirely run out.

I felt the beast's galloping approach in the floorboards. I glanced over my shoulder, saw it pelting toward me, its head swinging back and forth like a scythe. I leaped to my feet and dashed the remaining distance to the scissors. Then I swept them up and went very still, my back to the beast, watching it out of the corner of my eye. In the final moment before it gored me through the back, I whirled, lashing out with the scissors—

It knew my intent before I had even started moving. One arm caught me by the shoulder and slammed me to the floor. I thrashed, but its weight was enormous, pinning me, and suddenly I was underneath it and one of the faces in its belly, a pale little boy, began to whisper frantically, his dead eyes fixed on mine.

"Hello, girl," he said as I squirmed and screamed. "Make us a warm fire in the lands of the living, won't you? We're so very cold!"

An old woman's face nudged up close to his. "Have you seen Mary?" she asked. "I haven't seen her in months. I hope she's all right—"

And then all the faces began talking at once, gibbering, hissing, whispering of missing relatives, lost loves, of woes and aches and loneliness. A clawed foot slammed down inches from my head, embedding itself in the floor. Then the beast lowered its maw toward me, its breath washing over me, icy as winter's chill.

I could count all the beast's teeth, see right down its red, pulsing throat. But just when I was sure my last hour had come and it was going to eat me, the beast's eyes fixed on mine, and it said in the echoing voice of a woman, "Why have you brought us here? What sort of witch summons a soul eater into the lands of the living for sport?"

I stared up at those little glimmering eyes, too horrified to speak. Its voice had sounded furious, betrayed. "I . . . didn't . . . do it!" I wheezed, but the beast was not listening.

"You will pay for this, wicked thing. Are you not a Brydgeborn? Are you not supposed to be good and noble? Well, now you will join our merry company and whisper in the lands of the dead forever."

"Mrs. Cantanker?" I screamed. "Mrs. Cantanker, *what did you do?*"

But Mrs. Cantanker did not answer. I turned my face to the side, my hand worming into my pockets. My fingers closed around the locket. I gripped it with all my might, squeezing my eyes shut. I felt a terrible pinching sensation in my chest, as if all the breath and warmth were being dragged out of me.

"I'm sorry," I whispered. "I didn't do this. And I won't die for it."

I thought of the fireplace, of Mother and Papa, Teenzy and Vikers, Bram and Minnifer, of my friends at the orphanage, scratching their names into the comb. I thought of the trees in Pragast Wood, and the ghosts who were kind and did not bother anyone, and all the things in the world that were good.

There was a blinding flash of silver light. The windows in the gallery were flung open and a thousand flaming leaves burst in through the casements, a gust of wind whirling them around me and the beast and Mrs. Cantanker in a firestorm of russet, bronze, and red.

Mrs. Cantanker let out a cry. I was shouting too, my locket burning in my hand, but I did not let go. And as I lay on the floor, an enormous wave of power enveloped me, a glittering, screaming thing that burned in my veins, seeping outward until my skin felt strong and cold as armor.

The fangore went hurtling backward. I stood, my hair whirling around my face, the leaves slashing through the air. The fangore and all its many faces looked at me with horror, pain, and longing.

"Kaithus!" I shouted, raising the fist with the Anchor in it. "Go back. Go back so deep and far you will never find your way to the lands of the living again."

Its eyes widened, and suddenly I felt sorry for the creature, sorry that it had become tangled up in whatever game Mrs. Cantanker was playing. But there was no time for pity. I raised my scissors and drove them into the beast's shoulder. And then it was gone: a flicker, like a curtain, and the gallery was empty, only the autumn leaves remaining, strewn across the parquet.

I turned to Mrs. Cantanker, my heart beating very fast. Was she going to scold me, or fly at me in a rage? Now that the beast had failed to eat me alive, was she simply going to toss me out a window? But she did not seem angry. Her entire body was trembling, her eyes glittering. She seemed excited, *jubilant*.

"Well done," she said, brushing a lock of hair from

her face and straightening her cravat. "Well done, indeed. Your first fangore!"

"Mrs. Cantanker," I said, taking a few staggering steps toward her. "Why did you do that? Why did you bring a fangore here only to have me hurt it?"

"How else would you train?" she replied absently, and went to the writing desk, opening drawers and shuffling through papers. "It's all very normal, I assure you."

"But it's not allowed," I said. "We're not supposed to hurt things, not for sport."

She looked up at me sharply. "Oh, you are an expert, aren't you? Have you been reading books?" She smiled a sweet, cold smile. "Go on, little sparrow. Flutter off. Lessons are over, and I have *much* to do."

She lifted a finger and I was flung back, out the doors and down the corridor. I caught one last glimpse of Mrs. Cantanker's grinning face. Then the doors slammed shut.

I took a long bath in the great porcelain tub in the White Room. Boiling-hot water hissed from a snarl of brass pipes. I scooped copious amounts of lavender soaps and rose bath salts and pine bubble oils from buckets and jars, until the steam in the room was practically rainbow colored and thick as fog. Then I sank down so that the water came up to my nose and pondered, disturbing possibilities swirling in my head.

If Mrs. Cantanker had wanted me dead, she could have killed me months ago. The ghost of my old nanny had said they needed me in order to bring back Magdeboor. Was my guardian simply pretending to teach me to keep Mr. Grenouille from snooping, or to pass the time? But to pass the time until what? What was going to happen? What part was I playing in it? Or—and this thought made my stomach turn—what part had I already played?

I scrubbed all traces of the mandrake's heart and the fangore from my skin, changed into a comfortable blue dress, and went down to find Minnifer and Bram.

They were working, as usual, quietly and busily, Bram arranging cucumber shavings and little edible purple flowers on triangles of black bread, Minnifer presiding over her mountain of pillowcases with a butterfly net and looking very vicious, indeed. The triggles who'd been tasked to undo her work were now being forced to stitch up the pillowcases themselves, and they did so wth a great deal of mewling and complaining. They all looked up when I entered, little black eyes darting over me for anything shiny.

"Oh, hallo!" said Minnifer. "You're out early!" But then she saw my troubled face and slid down the pillowcase mountain, butterfly net in hand. "Are you all right? What happened?"

"I don't know," I said. "I think I did something very bad."

"We did hear a lot of crashing from upstairs," said Bram.

"We thought you must be having a very dreadful argument with a ghost," said Minnifer.

"We both bet you'd win, though," said Bram. "If it's any consolation."

I tried to ignore the unease nagging at the back of my

mind as I helped Bram and Minnifer with their chores. Once the triggles had finished their stitchery, we brought them out to the farthest corner of Pragast Wood to be released. Then we gathered mushrooms and berries from beneath the castle wall, and played tennis on the overgrown court, or tried to, though our rackets had no netting and we had only pine cones for balls. Finally we went down the valley to Hackenden village for groceries, shuffling through the frosty grass and blazing autumn leaves, and visited all the nicest shops. Folk pulled their children away when they saw us, and a few even crossed themselves and grew pale, but I hardly noticed.

Something is about to happen, I kept thinking, over and over again. *Something is about to change, and there's no going back now.*

It was evening by the time we returned to Blackbird Castle. The sun was peering moodily through the trees, like a red face through the bars of a prison. We were laughing as we came up the front steps, breathless from the cold and very hungry, pushing through the front doors. . . .

Mrs. Cantanker was waiting for us in the hall.

"Children!" she said, smiling down at us. She had changed into a peacock gown—splendid blue and purple and emerald satin—but she looked frazzled somehow, her grin too wide, her bejeweled fingers tapping quickly at her skirts. "I would like to introduce you to a friend of mine. He arrived just an hour ago and will be staying with us for a little while."

She stepped aside, revealing a small, knife-ish sort of man standing just behind her. He wore black riding boots and coattails cloven like the hoof of a goat. A slightly dirty polka-dot foulard had been knotted under his chin.

"Hello," he said, ignoring Minnifer and Bram and smiling a very foul yellow smile at me. "What a lovely house you have, Zita Brydgeborn."

Chapter Sixteen

I recognized him at once: it was the man I had glimpsed during my first week in Blackbird Castle, the one Mrs. Cantanker had let trundle off with a wheelbarrow full of paintings and silver. Up close, with those coattails and gleaming black boots, he looked rather like a postilion or a jockey. He wasn't badly dressed, but he struck me somehow as a grubby, unwholesome fellow. His skin was terribly pale, as if he had powdered it. His lips were red and shiny. He had the look of the men who loitered outside pubs and card dens, the ones who smoked too much and drank too much. He continued to smile at me, spinning an ebony cane against the floor like a top.

"Who are you?" I asked, Bram and Minnifer and I huddling together like frightened birds. "Did my mother know you?"

"They've met," Mrs. Cantanker snapped. "Not that it matters. Do not forget, Zita, that I am your guardian, and I will make the decisions in this house. I have spent *months* of my precious life teaching you the ways of witches while you whittled away at my last nerve. Now show a little gratitude. At the very least, show some manners."

I bristled. A voice in my mind was screaming, telling me to shove them both out the door and lock it behind them. But I felt cowed by their smiles and their hard, glittering eyes. I stole another glance at the man. With a start, I saw he had approached me very silently and was standing only a foot away, twirling his cane and admiring the grand hall. A cloud of some dark herbal perfume hung about him like a pall, and I could smell the cold of the outdoors on him too, and something a bit like chimney smoke.

"Gartlut's the name," he said, in a voice that was ever so elegant and refined, a voice that did not match his horrid yellow teeth at all. "And I assure you, Miss Zita, I'm no stranger here. In fact, you might call me a very old friend."

"Don't say anything," I said, pacing to and fro beneath the stargazing cupola. Minnifer and Bram were sitting atop a heap of cushions, looking anxious. Vikers was perched in the thicket of brass rods holding up the glass, surveying all three of us skeptically. "Don't even nod your heads unless you're sure it's safe to do. I'm going to tell you everything I've found out, and then we're going to make a plan."

I told Bram and Minnifer everything, then, about the vision I'd gotten from the treskgilliam tree, the blue rings with the spiders in them, and my fight with the fangore. I told them about the ghost of my old nanny, my memories of the Butcher of Beydun, and the whispers of Magdeboor's return.

"And as for Gartlut," I said. "A very old friend, my *foot*. He's no stranger here because he's been visiting in the night and stealing the silver. I saw him. He was making off with paintings and all sorts of treasures. And Mrs. Cantanker let him."

Bram and Minnifer were silent. Once again they reminded me of strange dolls, their legs trailing down the heap of cushions, their faces blank and sad. What was inside those enchanted heads? What would they tell me if they could? I wished I could help them, not just make them promises but *really* help them. I wished I were a powerful witch, and I wished Blackbird Castle had not fallen so far, that I hadn't returned only to have all the weight of its ruins placed on my shoulders.

"Can we go to Mr. Grenouille?" I wondered aloud, lying flat on the carpet and staring up at the stars. "Or to that other witch family in Manzemir? What if I told them everything I just told you?"

Minnifer giggled a weary, bitter giggle. "*They* wouldn't know what to do. And they wouldn't believe us either."

"Then we'll need proof," I said. "Unassailable proof that Mrs. Cantanker is part of a dastardly organization that is trying to bring high-ranking dead back from the spirit realm."

"But how will we get this proof?" Bram asked. "How will anyone ever believe us before it's too late?"

I sighed. In the blue bowl of the sky, the stars looked like some splendid, glittering meal that a giant scullery maid had forgotten to wipe away. They seemed very far away, winking and shining, and not caring at all for the troubles of an orphan and her friends. They made me feel adrift again, the way I had at Mrs. Boliver's and at the orphanage. I felt as if I were floating, surrounded by nothing but woods and ghosts, the looming mountains and the soft, indifferent gaze of those far-flung little lights.

And then I glanced over and saw that Bram and Minnifer had slid off the pile of cushions and had joined me on the floor. Even Vikers had flown from his perch to stand grimly next to my head.

"It might seem impossible," said Minnifer. "But you've been worse places than Blackbird Castle, haven't you, Zita? And so have we."

"Anyway, it just *seems* impossible," said Bram. "But it's a witch's house, after all, and nothing's ever quite what it seems. We'll find a way, or we'll try until there's no trying left."

I smiled at them. And we lay under the cupola and the vast starry night, discussing our predicament, while below us the castle creaked and groaned, as if it wanted to join our rebellion, as if it had sensed the new inhabitant scurrying in its guts and did not approve of him at all.

Winter crept slowly through Pragast Wood, prowling around the castle, reaching frosty fingers between the thick velvet drapes, chilling our feet when we woke in the morning and freezing our noses at night. By the end of November, it had arrived in earnest, lashing the windows with snow and sending tiles and weather vanes tumbling down the steep roofs. Lightning and thunder shuddered in the sky above the mountains. The trees could be heard creaking at night, their high, thin voices echoing across the gardens. Minnifer, Bram, and I battened down the hatches, spending as much time as possible by the great fire in the servants' hall.

My lessons with Mrs. Cantanker stopped altogether. She paid no attention to me or the servants, and spent all her time with Gartlut, giving him tours of the various strange and magical rooms, sitting in the cozy armchairs in the High Blackbird's study with piles of books around their feet, and sometimes disappearing for hours at a time. The household ghosts barely showed themselves anymore, cowering in corners and watching all this unfold with alarm.

In my mother's study, the fish that looked like they were on fire sank to the bottom of the aquarium, fading until they looked like lumps of coal. And as for the purple-winged moth, Mrs. Cantanker had carved it open. I crept into the tower room one evening to find it on a table, its golden blood draining into tubes for a potion. I'd been too horrified for words and had taken it out into a courtyard and buried it in the snow.

There was no cheer in the castle as we approached Christmas—only dread, as if some great terror were looming just around the bend. I could not yet make out its shape, but I could see its shadow stretching toward me. Sometimes I thought the shadow was Gartlut's. Sometimes I thought it was Magdeboor's. And sometimes I thought it was my own shadow that terrified me so, or the shadow of someone very like me, who I did not ever want to meet.

As for Gartlut, when he was not with Mrs. Cantanker, he was snooping. I could always tell where he had been because he had the bad habit of spitting on the floor, and would leave a nasty, glimmering trail wherever he went. I saw him out in the woods sometimes, or in the High Blackbird's study, his boots on my mother's desk. I hated him. Vikers hated him. Bram and Minnifer hated him most of all, and a shadow passed over their faces whenever he was near.

Gartlut seemed to hate us too. He showed it in the

roundabout way some people have, lavishing far too much attention on us whenever our paths crossed. He would want to discuss the weather, or ask us what we thought of the rooms we found ourselves in, whether the ceilings were well painted or ugly, and always he would find some small way to insult us or tip us ever so slightly off-balance. Meeting him was like meeting a cloud of buzzing insects on a hot summer day: you inevitably came out the other side feeling grimy and a little bit startled. One night he wandered into the servants' hall while we were eating supper, swinging his ebony cane and smirking. Our conversation broke off and we picked awkwardly at our food, waiting for him to go away.

"The cake was ghastly, Bram," he said, and Bram stared at him in surprise. "And Minnifer, dearie, I thought I told you I wanted my socks mended with little red roses, and it simply looks like the yarn caught the pox, red blotches all over them. It's shoddy work, really. Lazy work."

I shot out of my chair. Bram had worked hard on the cake, and Minnifer was too busy with Mrs. Cantanker's endless list of chores to be mending anyone's socks with roses. But both Bram and Minnifer remained seated, very still, looking down at their plates, their faces pinched and pale.

"You don't need to talk to them like that," I snapped. "They're doing you a favor, and they don't owe you a thing. Anyway, I tried that cake, and it was the best cake you'll find in the world."

Gartlut looked at me with amusement, one ink-black eyebrow arched. "The world?" he said. "The whole world? And what would you know of the world? You spend so much time down here with the servants that soon no one will be able to tell the difference. Ysabeau and I might sack *you* by accident."

My face reddened. I dug my nails into my palms, feeling like a thorn bush sprouting out of the floor. *"You,"* I said slowly, "have no right to be doing any sacking. And neither has Mrs. Cantanker. And if the work Bram and Minnifer do isn't good enough for you, you can leave."

I wished I had better words. I wished I could make Gartlut feel small and hurt, the way he had made Bram and Minnifer feel. But Gartlut only flashed his hideous smile and plucked a pastry from a platter, popping it into his mouth.

"That's no way to treat a guest," he said, chewing while he spoke and blowing crumbs all over the tablecloth. "But of course there were no fine airs or good graces locked up in those lovely bank accounts you inherited, were there? One never inherits the things one truly needs. One must find those all by one's self. And I don't think you're nearly clever enough to do that."

My face grew redder still. I wanted to fly at him and beat him over the head with a pan, but he was already turning away, flicking crumbs at me from his fingertips.

"Do not be so proud, little witch," he said. "And do not be so insolent. We all go to the same place one day, and we meet all sorts of people there who we never expected we'd see again. I'd watch myself."

Before I could retort, he left us, slipping out the door and closing it softly behind him.

That night I lay awake, listening to an owl hooting in Pragast Wood. The moonlight streamed in brightly, casting strange shadows across my comforters.

"That's no way to treat a guest," Gartlut had said, but he was no guest of mine. *I* was the guest now—no, less than a guest, an intruder—and both Gartlut and Mrs. Cantanker took every opportunity to make me feel it. I washed my own clothes and did my own ironing, and I was never asked to eat with Gartlut and Mrs. Cantanker in the Amber Room. Sometimes, when I walked past and saw them inside, whispering and laughing and reading their pamphlets in front of the fire, Mrs. Cantanker would rise and close the door in my face. I told myself I didn't care. I didn't want to spend a single moment with them anyway. But at the same time, it was horrifying to be made a stranger in your own home. I might have demanded my place. Now I feared it was too late.

I thought of running away. It would be easy enough to pack my things, take a handful of jeweled trinkets from Greta's study and sell them in the valley for a train ticket. I could go anywhere, buy a smart new dress and get a job in some great city where witches and ghosts seemed very far away. But it would only be *seeming*. I could not unsee the sights I had witnessed here, or unlearn the danger. I would still glimpse the darting will-o'-the-wisps, the ghostly cats, and the occasional hulking moorwhistler, and I'd remember all the spirits pressing against the veil, and all the work the Brydgeborns had done to preserve the balance of things, all of it ending with a little witch who had decided to run away. . . .

I looked at Vikers, dozing atop my bedpost, then righting himself abruptly, bristling his feathers and puffing out his chest. I thought of Bram and Minnifer down in the servants' hall, sleeping by the fire. *They* were all doing their part to set things right.

No, Zita, I told myself firmly. *You're not giving up.* It was easy to begin things, easy to end them too, but to make everything in between make sense . . . that was the challenge.

I let out a great puffy sigh and sank back into my pillows, staring up at the little painted cornflowers on the ceiling, the clouds and winged beasts. My gaze followed a blue ribbon, from painted hand, to knuckled tree branch, to the beak of a blackbird. And suddenly a memory slipped into my mind. It was just a soft thing—early spring, bright sunlight streaming through tree branches, Teenzy running after sticks, and my parents walking with me, my hands in theirs—but it calmed me, soothing as a gentle balm. The locket was warm against my skin, and I wrapped my hand around it, remembering my mother and father.

They would have fought for Blackbird Castle, I thought. *And they would have wanted me to fight for it too. I wanted more from life than dusting for Mrs. Boliver. Well, I've got it now, and so I'm going to rescue my family, break Bram and Minnifer's enchantment, reestablish Blackbird Castle as a beacon against the darkness—*

I was just beginning to feel utterly determined and full of righteous fury when I heard the sound of someone passing quickly by my room. I sat up abruptly. Then I crawled out of bed and tiptoed across the cold floorboards, opening the door a crack. I was just in time to see a globe of light vanish around the corner at the end of the corridor, along with the rustling plumage of Mrs. Cantanker's dressing gown.

Without a second thought, I darted out of my bedroom and followed, quick as a hare. Mrs. Cantanker's footsteps never slowed, nor did she look back over her shoulder. She swept past the doors to the greenhouse, the Parlor of Psychosis, the Room of Marble Heads, went up a flight of stairs and down another. And then I recognized where we were: the picture gallery, the one where Minnifer, Bram, and I had stood all those months ago, peering up at the painting of Magdeboor. Mrs. Cantanker went to its very end, raising her candle high. She whispered a word. . . .

I froze. There were the blue stairs again, the panel

slightly ajar. Without a moment's hesitation, as if she'd done it a thousand times, Mrs. Cantanker hitched up her dressing gown and began climbing toward Magdeboor's forbidden chambers.

I waited for her to scream, to come galloping back down chased by a swarm of weeshts and ghouls. But all I heard was the wind rattling the windowpanes and the sound of her footsteps echoing away. The realization that I was alone in the gallery crashed over me like an icy wave. I shuddered, drawing my nightgown around me. Then, avoiding Magdeboor's sharp black stare, I turned and fled back to my room.

Chapter Seventeen

WE were not idle the following weeks. In fact, our secret rebellion became quite busy now that winter was keeping us indoors. One morning Bram slipped a bit of star root into Mrs. Cantanker's and Gartlut's coffee, and then, while they snored facedown in their eggs and bacon, we searched the High Blackbird's study, Mrs. Cantanker's suite of rooms, even the little writing desk in the training hall.

We were hoping to find the sinister pamphlets Mrs. Cantanker read, letters to the spirits of the underworld, detailed modi operandi scribbled in journals, admittances of soul eating and summoning fangores for sport, and anything at all about the League of the Blue Spider and their plans to call the Dark Queen from beyond the veil. I entertained fantasies of bringing a great heap of proof to Mr. Grenouille and plopping it onto his desk in a cloud of dust.

But though we searched high and low, we found nothing. The writing table in the training hall had been swept clean, the High Blackbird's study as well, and as for the many drawers in my mother's great desk, they could not be opened at all. Their bulbous eyes had closed, lids pinched tightly shut, as if they were all wincing in pain.

I began to think increasingly about the blue staircase, about Mrs. Cantanker's skirts whispering away into the gloom. Was that where she and Gartlut were hatching their plans? I saw the stairs from time to time, at the end of passageways or half hidden in the corners of rooms. One evening I came across them in the corridor next to the pantry and stood for a moment, staring up them. I thought I heard sounds drifting from somewhere high above, the murmur of a distant wind, and oddly enough, the lapping of water.

"Are you intrigued?"

I spun. Gartlut was leaning against the wall, grinning his yellow grin.

"Best not be *too* intrigued," he said, twirling his ebony cane. "And best not go snooping. Not up there. Not a little witch like you."

I gave him my coldest, hardest glare and stalked away, but I was frightened more than anything. Where did those stairs *really* go? And had I imagined it, or had there been what looked like the tip of a long pale finger sticking out of the corner of Gartlut's mouth?

On December 19, the holiday of Saint Vulpine the Fallen, Mrs. Cantanker ordered a great feast. I was not invited. I wasn't sure anyone had been invited, except Gartlut and Mrs. Cantanker herself, though you might have been fooled by the number of dishes she demanded from the kitchens.

Minnifer and Bram were forced to cook from dawn till dusk, delicacies fit for a hundred nobles. I wanted desperately to retreat to Greta's library, but I was not about to leave my friends to do all the work on their own. I ran stacks of china to the great ballroom, dusted away the cobwebs, polished silverware, and helped Minnifer uproot flowers from the greenhouse for bouquets. I stirred soups and gravies, and tried to convince Bram to put floor sweepings and beetles into them, though he was far too proud of his work to do so. Then I stoked the great fire in the ballroom until it roared, and we all paraded up the stairs from the kitchens, bent double under the weight of silver trays and steaming tureens. By evening we were exhausted, our bones aching, our faces red from the blaze of the stoves.

I was just returning from delivering the last little pot of lobster consommé, steam slicking my face and gravy all down my apron, when I spotted Mrs. Cantanker descending the dragon staircase. Gartlut was with her, looking as grubby and supercilious as ever. But it was

Mrs. Cantanker I stopped to stare at. She was dressed in bloodred satin, a thousand ruffles dripping down the stairs behind her. Her face was powdered bone white. And she had dyed her hair black as a raven's wing, black like mine, like Mother's . . . like a Brydgeborn.

What *was* she playing at?

Both Mrs. Cantanker and Gartlut paused to look down their noses at me.

"And what are you doing in the front hall looking like a smudge of grime?" Mrs. Cantanker demanded. "Go back downstairs, before the guests arrive."

"What guests?" I asked, not moving an inch. I hadn't meant to confront her, but her calling me a smudge of grime made my temper rise and my fists clench. "Does Mr. Grenouille know you're throwing parties? Does he know you've stopped teaching me, and aren't being any sort of guardian at all?"

Mrs. Cantanker's eyes widened. Then she laughed musically, and linking arms with Gartlut, continued her descent. As they passed me, Mrs. Cantanker stopped, looking at me out of the corner of one eye.

"Mr. Grenouille knows whatever I want him to know," she said, her voice soft and sweet as spun sugar. "And Zita dear? Do not provoke me. Do not twitter and bite. You may think yourself a witch. You may think yourself ever so noble and brave. But you're still such a little bird. Just a sparrow. And the ravens and blackbirds feed on sparrows like you." She leaned down, her perfume so rich and noxious it made my eyes water. "I'll eat you up," she whispered, flashing a sharp red smile. Then she whirled away, and she and Gartlut marched toward the ballroom arm in arm, their shoes click-clicking on the marble like clocks.

"Who *are* they?" Minnifer asked, standing on a chair, which stood atop an overturned cauldron, and straining to look out one of the kitchen windows.

We had taken turns, but all we could see were legs, trooping up the front steps and into the castle. Some of them were regular human legs in trousers and winter velvets. But I could have sworn some of them bent in odd directions, and some seemed to be clustered together as if a little family was hurrying along in a tight huddle. Those huddles were always accompanied by a faint skittering sound, the clicking of joints and pincers on stone, and sharp, warbling voices.

"I don't know," I said, holding the chair so it wouldn't slip off the cauldron. "But I don't think we have any time left."

Moments before we were to ring the dinner gong, Mrs. Cantanker swept into the servants' hall, brandishing a great key in her hand. "Bon appétit," she said, just before locking us in. "And don't be dozing off. There'll be loads of dishes to wash come midnight."

We ate our supper in silence, picking at the crusts and clippings left over from the grand dishes. Occasionally we heard noises from upstairs, the rumple of feet and ringing peals of laughter.

I fed Vikers crumbs and bits of steak from a saucer. And then, when I felt the dinner must be well under way, I went to the door. The leaf-shaped tines of Greta's skeleton key shimmered as I slipped them into the lock.

"Zita?" said Bram, glancing at me. "Where are you going?"

"Upstairs," I said. "*All* the way upstairs. Mrs. Cantanker and Gartlut are going to be in the ballroom for ages, what with all the food they've got to gobble through. So I'm going to find out what's at the top of the blue staircase."

Bram set down his fork slowly. Minnifer half rose from her chair. "The blue stairs?" she demanded. "Are you mad?"

"Zita, you can't," said Bram. "We've no idea where those stairs go."

"Because we haven't gone up them," I said stoutly. "But I'm going to. And I was hoping you both would come with me, at least to the bottom, just in case I need help or the feast ends early—"

"You know people died up there?" Minnifer said, coming round the table to confront me. "One of the

Brydgeborn children wandered up those stairs a hundred years ago to look for a lost toy and was never seen again. Except for his hair. Every year on the day of his disappearance, a letter was sent from the spirit realm containing one black curl."

I shuddered, but I said, "I don't believe a word of it. A few days ago, I saw Mrs. Cantanker go up those stairs, and *she's* still very much alive. And then Gartlut told me not to snoop there, which if you ask me is practically like posting a great sign that says 'We're hiding something right here.' If there's proof of their plans anywhere, it's at the top of those stairs. So are you coming or not?"

Minnifer stayed rooted to the floor. Bram shifted, chair legs creaking. I beckoned Vikers, but even he looked hesitant and became suddenly busy with a bit of gristle.

"Fine," I said. "Stay. But if I die, or Mrs. Cantanker catches me, I've resolved to haunt you all for a good long while, and put snails in your pillowcases."

I turned and hurried out of the servants' hall with as much bravado as I could muster. It was with great relief that I heard footsteps and flapping behind me, for I would have died of fright having to face what lay ahead alone.

Chapter Eighteen

WE went to my chambers first. I equipped myself with my witch's belt. Bram and Minnifer rifled through Greta's things and stuffed their pockets with lavender sachets and protective salt-and-silver charms. Then we lit a pair of lamps and crept off in search of the blue stairs. It did not take long to find them. They were in the picture gallery again, their little panel standing ajar. I had the impression they were *lurking*, like something living, some small animal, coiled malevolently next to the Antechamber of Eternal Dreams.

The air grew icy as we approached. Vikers perched on

my shoulder, grim and alert. Bram and Minnifer were silent, but I could feel their fear, prickling like spiders across my neck.

"If anyone comes, whistle," I said as we gathered at the foot of the stairs. "And then run."

"We're going up with you," said Minnifer, but I shook my head.

"You keep watch. I'll take my chances with the spirits of the underworld, but I *don't* want to get caught by Mrs. Cantanker and Gartlut when I'm elbow-deep in a pile of evidence. I've got my locket and my belt. I'll find my way back."

They both nodded unhappily. Then Minnifer hugged me, and I was so surprised I stood very stiffly, like a hat stand. Then I hugged her back. "Thanks," I said quietly. "I don't know what I'd do without you two."

With that, I lifted my lamp and stepped onto the blue stairs. Immediately, I felt Vikers fly from my shoulder. I glanced back and saw he had landed in a chandelier and was watching me keenly. I tried to look encouraging and brave for the benefit of Bram and Minnifer, but I don't think I succeeded. Their eyes only widened further, and Minnifer looked as if she was about to run after me and haul me back. I took another step, then another. Before I could change my mind, I clattered up several steps very quickly, out of sight of my friends.

The darkness was almost complete. It pressed around me, chewing at the lamplight as if trying to swallow it whole. At first I imagined I heard noises, the flap of wings, taunting voices, and once again the lick and gurgle of water. In my head, red-eyed beasts and gargoyles were congregating with buckets of hot tar. But it was probably only doves, bats, triggles, and leaking pipes.

They're just stairs, I told myself sternly. *Regular stairs, that happen to be painted blue, and might lead to the lair of an ancient dark witch, but you don't* know *that.*

And yet the farther I climbed, the more my courage began to waver. The stairs turned this way and that, traveling much higher than I would have thought possible. The blue paint began to scab and peel, becoming

blackened with soot. A curious smell tickled my nose—
ash and cinders and green stagnant water. And then I
came to the top and paused, my heart beating very fast.

I was looking down a long, low passageway. By my
calculations it should have been somewhere under the
roof, and yet it felt somewhere else entirely. The walls
were built of heavy stone, mossy and slick with mois-
ture. Tendrils of fog slipped over the floor. At the corridor's end, small and dark and studded with nails, was a
little crooked door.

I took several steps toward it, my feet squelching
through mushrooms and rot. There were no cobwebs
here. No bats or mouse droppings. The sound of water
was louder now. I had the horrible feeling that I was no
longer quite where I thought I was, that if I turned, I
would see not the stairs but that mossy passage stretching on forever.

I reached for my locket, gripping it fiercely, and started
down the corridor at a brisk clip. Out of the corner of
my eye, I thought I saw spiny shadows racing along the

walls, whispering and hissing. I began to run, stumbling on the uneven flagstones, and I was sure I glimpsed Teenzy up ahead, blurry and sad eyed, watching me from the threshold of the crooked door. My lamp slipped from my fingers, extinguishing in the muck. I did not stop. From somewhere far away, I heard a rumbling, like many running feet. . . . Then I was at the door. Teenzy was gone. I pushed through, slamming the door behind me and shutting my eyes tight.

It was the water that made me look up. I was up to my ankles in it. It wasn't warm or particularly cold. A dank, moldy sort of wind blew against my cheeks. I found myself looking across a vast, practically endless marsh. The sky was very dim, not quite night and not quite day, but a dreary, unchanging twilight. There were no stars, no moon. In fact, it was less a sky than a ceiling, as if the marsh was underground, in an enormous chamber. Golden lamps floated here and there, glittering in the water.

I looked back. The door stood alone, just a frame on

a tiny lumpen island, and nothing behind it but more marshland as far as the eye could see.

What on earth? I thought. But I knew that earth had nothing to with it. I had crossed over. I was in the Kingdom Between.

All was silent except for the shush of the wind and the soft lapping of the water. Up ahead, standing atop a grassy protuberance, was a small cottage. No smoke rose from its crooked chimney. It looked long abandoned. I began picking my way across the marsh toward it, leaping from tuft of grass, to hillock, to rock, my locket held high in one hand. It gave off a soft glow, surrounding me in a silver haze.

Ghosts drifted in the mist, figures in little boats with little lanterns. One passed quite near, and I saw that the lantern did not have a flame inside it, but a letter, glowing warmly in a glass globe. *To Mr. Hilliam, my dearest friend,* I read. Other ghosts were on foot, moving steadily into the gloom. Some held candles, or radiant little mementos. Some had almost no light at all. And from far away, where the marsh met the sky in a bloody band, I heard a terrible howling, screeching, and unearthly roars.

One of the ghosts spotted me and drifted closer, her gaze imploring. She might have been thirty if she'd been alive. Her dress was old-fashioned, threadbare and checkered, and though she had no candle or lamp, she held a dried-up flower in one hand that gave off the tiniest flickering spark. "Are you a Blackbird?" she whispered. "They are going to eat me if you do not help me. I have such a little light. I will never get past them!"

I nodded, but I didn't slow my pace. "I'll give you a coin," I said, fiddling with one of the purses on my belt. "But that's all I can do—"

The air began to crackle, growing chilly. The ghost was drawing closer and closer still. And then, without warning, she scrabbled at me, grasping for my locket and its brilliant silver light.

A wave of arctic cold crashed against me. "No!" I shouted, wrenching away. "That's mine! That's *my* family!"

"But I *want* it," she snarled, and her face twisted, a wart sprouting from her forehead and a long, sharp fang poking over her lip. I felt along the sachets of herbs on my belt, my fingers feeling the little emblems on their drawstrings. *Rosemary attracts, lavender repels, wormwood cloaks from unwanted attention . . .*

I dug the wormwood from its sachet and threw a handful into the air, darting through the falling flakes and begging them with all my strength to make me invisible. The wormwood seemed to oblige, because the woman lost her grip on me and stood very still, gazing about with a hungry, bereft expression. I ran, splashing through the green waters and clambering up the bank to the cottage. I looked back over my shoulder and caught a glimpse of her, knee-deep in the water, her little flower sparking feebly, and something drawing nearer in the darkness, something with many legs and many eyes. Then I pushed through the rotting door and stumbled into the cottage.

Inside, all was blackness. I held my locket high,

illuminating what looked to be a warren of small chambers, fitted together at odd, uneven angles. Signs of witchery lay everywhere: a tall mirror in a gilt frame, a scrying globe, baskets of dried plants and roots, heaps of parchments and books. Nothing like the fine bronze and silver instruments in my mother's study, however. These were dark things, skulls and iron pincers and bottles filled with pickled eyeballs. Did they belong to Mrs. Cantanker? Or Magdeboor?

I took a few tiny, terrified steps, my locket cutting into my fingers. I tried to imagine what Greta would do in this situation. Most likely she would have swept in much more bravely than me, not a strand of hair out of place, her black shoes polished bright enough to blind. She would not have been afraid.

I am a witch of Blackbird Castle, I thought. *Last of my line. And I can do this as well as anyone.*

I passed towers of books, a bed with a red curtain, birdcages, their inhabitants long gone. The floor was crowded with buckets to catch drips from the leaky roof, and I picked my way carefully between them, my shoes sliding like boats through narrow channels.

By the third room, I began to suspect that many of the things in the cottage had been taken from Blackbird Castle. I saw stacks of oil paintings, photographs, even the silver-framed pictures I'd seen lying facedown on my mother's desk. What were those doing here? And then I came to the farthest room in the cottage, and there, sitting sideways to me, on a chair beneath a low window, was Greta.

She was humming softly, hunched over something in her lap. A spool of red thread lay on the floor by her feet, and she clutched a needle in one hand, dipping it up and down, up and down. I almost called out to her. But something stopped me.

What was Greta doing *here*? I closed my fist around my locket and drew back into the shadows.

A ghost passed outside the window, its lantern shining briefly through and illuminating what Greta was holding. It was a doll. Its limbs were long and gangling, and its wax face wore a rather melancholy expression. Another doll lay by Greta's foot, smaller, with a bun of brown hair. Bram and Minnifer. Bram and Minnifer in doll form, button-eyed and boneless. And as I watched, Greta began stitching Bram's mouth shut with bright red thread.

I remained perfectly still, watching the needle flash. When Greta had finished both dolls, she tossed them carelessly onto the sill and turned, drifting toward me. I shrank farther into the dark, willing the wormwood enchantment to hide me. She passed by without a sound, out of the cottage and across the marsh toward the distant door into Blackbird Castle. She held no light like the other ghosts, but nothing came near her or disturbed her journey. It was almost as if they were afraid of her.

As soon as she was gone, I ran to the dolls, snipping the stitches with my silver scissors and pulling them out as gently as I could. Then I whirled through the room, opening drawers, upending baskets, my mind churning.

Greta was one of them? Greta was a member of the League of the Blue Spider?

But it couldn't be. She had been helping me! She had given me the skeleton key and the waking spell and had shown me the way to the secret library!

I forced myself to stop and breathe. *Find proof of Magdeboor's return and get out of here, Zita. You'll have time to think later.*

Kneeling, I rifled through heaps of ancient papers, crawled under a table, one broken leg propped up with a skull. Sheaves of letters had been stacked there, some of them from hundreds of years ago, scrawled so viciously I could not begin to decipher them, and each signed with a large black M. But I found newer letters too, in creamy envelopes, tied into bundles with black silk ribbons.

Dear Mrs. Cantanker Harkleath-St. Cloud,

Our faction was delighted to hear of the heir's return to Blackbird Castle. I told them of it at our quarterly meeting, and it caused much celebration. I trust you are putting everything in place for the final summoning? You will have no trouble tricking the girl. You say she was raised an orphan? Then she is utterly unaware of the things with which we occupy ourselves and no doubt quite stupid. . . .

I gritted my teeth, opening the envelopes one by one and sliding out the messages.

The Butcher was here this evening; he stepped from the fireplace, and we spoke many hours with him in the upstairs parlor. Magdeboor sends her greetings. She was never a patient creature, but never so impatient as now. . . .

I stuffed the letters into my cloak, bundle after bundle, not bothering to read them all. No one would be able to see these and not understand what evil schemes Mrs. Cantanker had been hatching. When my pockets were as full as I could stuff them, I clambered to my feet and was about to flee the cottage, when something else caught my eye: on the floor, half hidden among scrolls and garlands of rotting greenery, sat a red satin box.

I knelt, opening it quickly. Inside was a collection of household records. I saw lists of accounts with butchers and dressmakers, long rows of wages for people I had never heard of. It was not what I needed, or so I thought, and I would have closed it again when I spotted a photograph tucked among the papers. I lifted it, brushing the dust away. It showed the servants of Blackbird Castle, assembled on the front steps. It must have been taken long ago, when there were still parties on the lawn and my mother entertained dignitaries in the drawing room and royalty in the banquet hall. But no, there was a date scribbled in one corner. It had been taken just last year.

I searched the photograph for Minnifer and Bram. I couldn't find them. And then my heart stopped.

They were all in a row: Mother, Greta, and John Brydgeborn. Only they were not wearing the grand clothes they'd had on in the dining room. Greta wore a maid's cap. John was dressed as a gardener, his spectacles still on his nose, a leather apron down his front. Above each figure was a name and an occupation.

Mrs. Hanguard, housekeeper

Flora Wheeler, chambermaid

Andrew Craik, dogsbody

My mind took several stuttering seconds to realize what I was seeing. Then everything clicked into place and I pushed the box away from me as if it had bitten me.

The missing pictures on the walls, so that I wouldn't know the difference between a family member and a stranger.

The clothes in Greta's closet, for someone small, though the golden-haired ghost was tall and lovely.

Mother looking quite different in the dining room than she did in my locket, and the reason why the waking spell had not worked . . . could never, ever have worked.

The bodies propped up in the dining room, dressed in lace and velvet, were not my family's. And everyone— Mrs. Cantanker, Greta, even Minnifer and Bram—was lying.

Chapter Nineteen

I bolted out of the cottage, the red satin box under my arm, letters flying from my cloak pockets and drifting into puddles and ponds. I felt sick and faint, my sweat turning to an icy sheen on my forehead.

Greta wasn't Greta at all, but the ghost of someone named Flora Wheeler, a servant girl who had been murdered in Greta's place. The bodies in the dining room were pawns in this wicked game, perhaps even members of the League of the Blue Spider, eager to sacrifice themselves for their Dark Queen's return. But then where *were* the Brydgeborns? And who were Bram and Minnifer?

They certainly had not been servants here since they were little, not if they weren't even in a picture from last year. I wondered suddenly if they had been reporting to Mrs. Cantanker this entire time, passing on every bit of news and every development.

The gallery was empty when I arrived at the bottom of the blue stairs. Vikers was no longer in the chandelier. Bram and Minnifer were gone too, only the faintest haze of lamp smoke signaling they had been there at all.

It's like they know, I thought. *It's like they know I've discovered they're all liars, and now they've run away.*

I pounded down the servants' staircase, making straight for my room. My old carpetbag was still under the bed, untouched since the day I arrived: my Sunday bonnet, the lump of soap, the comb with my friends' names scratched into the handle. I dragged it out, dumping the red box and all the letters into it. Then I crept down the dragon staircase and out the front doors.

The cold that greeted me on the front steps was so bitter it shocked me a moment. Wind and snow howled out of the sky. My hat almost blew from my head, and I had to gather my carpetbag under one arm and hold the rest of me together with the other. I thought of whistling for Vikers, but suddenly I wasn't sure. I wasn't sure of anything anymore, or anyone, and it felt horribly, horribly unfair. Why, if you trusted people, did they have to lie to you?

Faintly, I heard the tinkle of silverware and the thrum of voices. I turned, hesitantly, peering along the front of the castle. Then I plowed through the deep snow to one of the ballroom windows, betrayal bitter in my chest. Would Bram and Minnifer be in there, and Vikers? Had they all just been waiting for me to go away so they could celebrate too? If they were, at least I would know. I would know I had never had any friends here.

Warm, bright light spilled out into the darkness. For a moment I thought the steam from the fire had blurred the panes, but then I blinked and the glass was clear, and it was only my eyes, pricking and being disloyal. I wiped them and stood on tiptoes, pressing my nose against the icy glass. The ballroom was full of guests—human ones in fine suits and gowns, and dead ones too, ghosts of all shapes and sizes, sinuous barrow wights, muscle-bound moorwhistlers, and giant spidery gentlemen in red waistcoats.

Mrs. Cantanker sat at the head of the table, glittering and lovely. I didn't see Bram and Minnifer, or crows of any kind, but I did spot Gartlut, draped over a chair by the fireplace. His head was tipped back. His fingertips trailed on the floor. He looked as if he had been peeled off like a suit of clothes, or the rind of an orange. And who should be standing next to him, silhouetted against the raging fire in the hearth, but the Butcher of Beydun.

The dead king was exactly as I remembered him, exactly as he had been when he'd called to me from the woods—tall as a birch tree, thin as a fish bone, swaying like a wisp of candle smoke. As I watched, Mrs. Cantanker went to him and took his hand.

Together they glided to the center of the ballroom. They began to dance, the ghosts and villains whirling around them. A wild music kicked up, sounding of violins sawn in half, tin whistles broken across knees, clarinets screeching in dismay.

I was just about to turn from the snowy panes and make my way down into the valley when seven triggles, standing one atop the other, wobbled up behind me and struck me on the back of my head with a brick.

Chapter Twenty

I woke in a broom cupboard, my skirts wet and caked with blood and my shoes full of water. I had been dumped unceremoniously over a heap of boxes. My legs were sticking into the air, and my cheek was pressed to the dusty floorboards. The broom cupboard had a small, round window on the wall, and the gray dawn was streaming through it, glittering in the dust and puddles. It was morning; I must have been out for hours.

I was not normally the crying sort, but it was the first thing I did. I found a footstool to sit on, put my throbbing head in my hands, and in the tarnished silver light from the window, I wept.

I'd been an idiot, stopping to look into the ballroom. I'd been an idiot from the beginning, really, thinking that *I* was capable of becoming a Blackbird and a witch. What had made me think I could live in this place and become its mistress—me, an orphan from Cricktown? Blackbird Castle was not my home. Maybe it had been once, but it was not anymore. Gartlut had been right: one could not inherit the things I needed, nor find them in bank accounts. Perhaps I'd never been meant for any of this. Perhaps I'd never been meant for anything but brooms and dustpans and the low stone wall of Mrs. Boliver's garden.

I think I would have wept forever if I'd not felt the soft, warm glow of my locket flickering against my skin. My skeleton key had been taken from me. My pockets were empty and my witch's belt gone. No doubt the triggles had made quick business of that. But my locket was still clenched in my fist, and slowly, I opened my fingers, looking at the smiling family inside.

For Zita Brydgeborn, last of her name, I read, tracing the tiny writing around the frame. *May this light always guide you home.*

Papa seemed to wink at me. Mother smiled, sweet as summer lilies. Once again, I felt as though they could see me, that they were looking right out of the little silver frame, as through a window.

I smiled back, wishing with all my heart that they were here. And then, all at once, Mother rose and approached the glass.

I gasped. The image swirled like smoke, and suddenly she was no longer in a drawing room. She was standing in a twilit marsh, her ankles wreathed in mist. "Mother?" I whispered. "Oh, Mother . . ."

"Darling Zita," she said. "You must not give in."

"But I don't know what to do!" Tears were stinging my eyes, and I was shivering violently. "I thought I did. I thought I could fix all this, but it's too big and too difficult and no one is who they say they are. I suppose if I were like you, I could stop Mrs. Cantanker and the Butcher from summoning Magdeboor. But I'm not anything like you."

Mother's eyes grew sad. "And why," she asked, "should you be anything like me?"

"Because then I would be sure!" I almost shouted. "Then I would be sure I belonged here and wasn't just pretending. A witch is never unsure, but I am."

"A witch is never unsure?" Mother repeated thoughtfully. "Is that what Ysabeau has been teaching you? But a witch is always unsure. Life is unsure. It is like a candle flame, always flickering and changing. Only death and darkness are certain, and despite what people may think, those are not a witch's business. Daughter, even if you cannot see the truth of things, even if you are frightened and discouraged, know this: Some things just are. You don't have to be sure of them. They don't ask your opinion."

I sat up, chewing at the end of my braid. "Like what?"

"Like you! You're here, aren't you? You grew up to be a brave, extraordinary girl, despite being kidnapped by the Butcher King, despite living almost your entire life on your own. And even when you thought you were alone, you had parents who loved you and never stopped searching for you, and a whole world and a castle and a crow waiting for you." She smiled. "Those things are sure, Zita. Those things are true." And then her gaze hardened and she looked back over her shoulder. "But now you must hurry. Ysabeau will be calling Magdeboor soon. There is nothing I can do from here . . . but you can stop her, Zita. She's afraid of you. And well she should be."

"But how?" I asked. "Mother, tell me how—"

"The staircase," she said, and behind her in the gloom I saw something approaching, darting briskly from hillock to hillock. "They are cursed to sleep, but you can wake them. I sent Teenzy with the spell, left it for you in Greta's library. Wake the dragon stairs—"

"The waking spell!" I gasped. It had never been for the people in the dining room. It had been for the dragon stairs! "And then what? Mother, then what?"

But there was only the room again behind the glass, the fireplace, and Teenzy on a cushion, and my parents' smiling faces.

I sat on the footstool, peering into the locket, my heart filled to the brim. And then, from far away, I heard a long, low horn, the thunder of hooves, and the tinkle of harnesses, echoing out of the valley. It drifted toward me through the branches of Pragast Wood, gentle and hopeful.

I sat up sharply, wiping my nose on my sleeve. And then I leaped to my feet and ran to the window. It was the post coach! Someone was coming to Blackbird Castle!

I began scrabbling about the broom cupboard, examining my options. Of course the cupboard was mostly full of brooms and dustpans, but also dusty cushions and iron candlesticks, feather comforters, and chairs with the wicker seats popped out—the sorts of things that collected in old houses and had to be put somewhere out of sight. I decided the best course of action would be to make a great deal of noise and then beat whoever came to investigate over the head with a candlestick. Choosing a suitably wicked-looking one from a dusty heap, I squeezed myself next to the door. Then I began to scream and kick with all my might, loud enough to make anyone who heard me think I was dying. I expected to hear running feet and anxious voices immediately, but there was no response.

I stopped, red-faced and perspiring. Again, I heard the sound of the post coach, but now the sound of its wheels was retreating, rumbling back down into the valley. That meant whoever was in it had been unloaded. They would be climbing up the path toward Blackbird Castle. . . .

I set down the candlestick and looked about. The window was narrow, but I was rather narrow myself. I suspected I could tip myself out of it.

I went to it and rattled the frame. It opened with a rasp, freezing air billowing into the room. Then I popped the window right out of its frame, wrenching it off its hinges, and looked down.

I was on the fourth floor, in a little gable right at the edge of the roof. I certainly wouldn't survive a jump. Nor could I climb. The ivy had given up about ten feet below me, only a few tendrils snaking around the broom cupboard's window. I could perhaps signal the visitor, or shout at them, or send a paper plane down with the message. . . .

I whirled back to the little room. A pile of frilly sheets and comforters lay stacked in one corner. It would be a cliché, using those, something straight out of one of Greta's fairy tales. If anyone ever bothered writing a book about me, the critics would say, "Tut-tut, it would have been more satisfying had she built a ladder out of chair legs and tied it together with her own hair." But I had no time to bother about that now.

I began knotting the sheets together, end to end, as tightly as I could. I tied the last comforter around the handle of the cupboard door. Then I shoved the whole mass out the window and stuffed myself out after it.

I got stuck halfway through. I imagined my legs flailing in the broom cupboard behind me, my front half hanging from the window as if the window were sticking out its tongue. But then I shot out, like a cork, and found myself tumbling through open air. I fell for so long

I wondered if I had tied the sheets up for nothing and was going to plummet all the way down to the ground. But then my hand caught a comforter, and I gripped it with both arms, and began to slide and dangle wildly downward.

I had imagined a graceful descent, a tense, silent journey, but the whole thing was more of a terrifying, controlled collapse. I felt the knots unraveling even as I descended—third floor, second floor, past the great windows in the drawing room, mercifully dark and curtained—and then the ground was rushing up to meet me. I fell the last five feet and landed with a *flump!* on a bank of fresh snow. The comforters landed on top of me, rather gently, as if they expected me to go to sleep.

I popped up at once and crawled from the snowbank, wild-eyed and desperate. Then I burst across the gardens, down the steps, and past the snow-covered shrubs, running as fast as I could for the narrow path that led into the woods. I must have looked a proper lunatic with my bloody brow and my hair all wild. Up ahead, I saw my savior, emerging from the trees: a little suitcase; a bright, cheery face with a perfectly round red spot on each cheek.

It was Mr. Grenouille!

"Zita!" he cried out in alarm, setting down his suitcase. "My dear girl, what has happened?"

I ran to him, practically tripping over him in my haste. "Mrs. Cantanker is in league with Magdeboor and the Butcher of Beydun," I said, looking back at the castle in terror. "And the bodies in the dining room aren't my family. They're servants. I don't know if anyone here is who they say they are, even Bram and Minnifer. . . . We need to get to Hackenden, and we need to get help—"

Mr. Grenouille turned a circle in the path, as if to see if anyone was nearby. Then his hand tightened around my wrist, his eyes turning small and black and buzzing, like a pair of flies.

Oh no. No no no. Not you too.

"My dear girl," said Mr. Grenouille, smiling at me. "You are confused! And you've got blood *all* over your face. Come, let me show you the way."

Chapter Twenty-One

MR. Grenouille half dragged, half shoved me back toward Blackbird Castle, though I fought and twisted every step of the way. He was far too strong for such a little man. I wondered how I had ever thought him good and honest.

He pulled me up the front steps and hammered on the door. A horrid creature opened it, goat-headed, talons like a bird, its hairy upper half stuffed into a grimy green waistcoat. The creature smelled as if it had been buried for years and had just been dug up, and even Mr. Grenouille looked unnerved as it ushered us into the hall.

All was shadowy, the wicks in the sconces unlit. The doors to the ballroom stood open, and the smell of stale food hung in the air. *Things* were drifting about, not household ghosts, but evil things from deep in the underworld. They lounged in the chandelier, skulked in and out of doorways. A ghoul, its skull green and rotting, ran chittering across the hall. Chairs were piled in corners, food and silver had been thrown across the tiles, and all of Minnifer's lovely flowers had been trampled on, their leaves and pink petals ground into the floor. Mrs. Cantanker was hurrying down the dragon staircase toward us, her eyes wide.

"Charles!" she exclaimed. "And Zita! Whatever has happened!"

"There is no need for artifice now," Mr. Grenouille said, twisting my arm and shoving me toward her. Even his voice was different, harsh and grating where before it had been weak. "She knows. Where's Gartlut?"

The change that came over Mrs. Cantanker was immediate. "Upstairs," she said, her face going cold as marble. "Preparing. It's about time you arrived, Charles. You missed an absolutely delightful feast last night in celebration of the dawn of our new age. The entire league was here."

I stole a look at the stairs. An enormous horned head formed the newel post. It was scaled and gilded, its jeweled eyes almost closed. *"Wake the dragon stairs . . ."*

I reached out, trying to brush a hand over its snout, but Mr. Grenouille jerked me back. "I was waylaid," he said, and up in the chandelier, a goblin snickered and began to swing back and forth, causing a rain of crystal beads to fall onto the tiles. "Am I the last?"

"Yes. And we might not have waited another day."

"You might have waited another year if I'd not come up when I did," snapped Mr. Grenouille. "Precious Zita was about to head off into the wild blue yonder, and then where would we be, hmm?"

"The spirits would have caught her before she was halfway through the woods," said Mrs. Cantanker coolly. "We are taking no risks, not now." She tipped her face up toward the ceiling, a dreamy, wild look in her eyes. "Magdeboor is waiting. Her feet are in the water, her gaze turned to these bright shores. We shall bring her back, smuggle her into the lands of the living . . . and you," she said, turning to me sharply. "You, I will thankfully never have to see again. I'm sick to death of you. Every day, every moment, I spent shepherding a servant girl through the hallowed traditions of witchery. . . . It made me want to scream."

"You *did* scream," I snapped. "A lot. And I don't know why you bothered teaching me anything, if you were just going to get rid of me." Anger boiled up inside me, and I could feel my cheeks growing red. I ceased to struggle against Mr. Grenouille's grasp and stood as straight as I could. "Why am I still alive if you hate me so much?"

Mrs. Cantanker sniffed. "Oh, you'll see. Very soon, Zita, all those years of work, all those secret meetings, dukes and lowly scullery maids sitting together, the wolves with the sheep, the League of the Blue Spider plotting to bring Magdeboor back . . . it's all about to be worth it. She will shatter the borders between life and death. She will restore the witches to their former glory, not those elegant, puffed-up creatures we have today, but *true* witches, strong and merciless and above all laws. No more pandering. No more playing nice."

I stared at her in disbelief. "What makes you think that will have anything to do with *you*? You're not even a witch!"

Mrs. Cantanker's eyes flashed. For a moment I thought she might throttle me on the spot. But then she seemed to regain control of her features and smiled a brittle smile. "Did the servants tell you? I knew I ought not to have spared them. . . . But yes! So what? I'm not a witch, not in the traditional sense. I cannot see the dead. I can do only the most primitive magic."

Her voice became a snarl. "But listen well, *Zita Brydgeborn*, before you dare think your ratty little self above me. I worked and I *toiled* to become what I am. I made myself strong and clever, cleverer than any of the others, cleverer than your mother. And was I ever good enough for your lot? No! Because I was not born into the proper family. Because I did not have the right blood. Well, guess what, *Georgina*," she spat, as if my mother were standing in the hall with us. "I found my own path, despite your urgings, despite you saying I should become a professor or a polite little historian. 'Don't go that way,' you said. 'Don't go places that will lead you into darkness.' But the darkness takes everyone. The darkness wasn't too good to have me."

She spun, her skirts swirling. She was still dressed in the bloodred gown from the night before, only it was in need of steaming and ironing, and her hair was falling out of its pins. Her voice was venomous as she paced the checkerboard tiles. "It will all turn out in the end, though. Who do you think Magdeboor will be beholden to when she returns? You and your ilk, who have kept her imprisoned in the underworld for centuries? Or me, who freed her? I think I will reap quite handsomely for my labors, thank you very much. And all the lazy witches of this world in their gilt drawing rooms and summer mansions, and the fat old kings who think themselves above us, and everyone who ever laughed at me when I failed. . . . They will be dead."

Her fingers were knotted in front of her, so tightly they'd turned warped and bloodless. Her eyes glittered. I imagined her suddenly as a child, red-haired and freckled, a frightened girl at some illustrious magic school, unable to perform even the simplest spell, unable to see the ghosts that tickled across her forehead or hung menacingly behind her in the dark. This was what had grown in that bitter, lonely soil: a magnificent creature, but so full of vengeance and hate. For a moment I felt sorry for her.

But only for a moment. "I'll never help you summon Magdeboor," I said. "You can kill me if you want, but I'll not bring her back."

"Oh, Zita," said Mrs. Cantanker, and all around us, the lingering beasts and spirits began to chuckle and laugh, horns bobbing and black eyes flashing. "It's too late for that. You've already summoned her! You, our last little key to Magdeboor's locks and chains. You broke them open one by one. Banish a ghost whose sins on earth are not yet forgiven? You did that in the Black Sitting Room on your very first day. Change the natural course of the weather for no reason at all? Done. Kill a fangore for sport? Done. All of these things are very much forbidden to an honorable witch. But then you wouldn't know that, would you? Because you're nothing but a housemaid, all dressed up. . . ."

Except I'm not, I thought. *Some things just* are, *and I'm a Blackbird.*

Mrs. Cantanker approached me and lifted my chin, exactly as she had on the night I'd met her. I had been frightened then, awed by her flashing looks and grandeur, but I was not fooled by those things now. I knew what she was, and I looked her coldly in the eye.

"So proud," she murmured, digging one long red nail into my skin. "But what are you *really*, Zita? Cinders and sparrows. Cinders and sparrows, where I am fire and crows. You are no match for me. We have one more task for you, one more key to twist. And then I'm afraid your usefulness will have entirely run out."

She turned to Mr. Grenouille, who was leaning against the dragon-head newel post, his elbow poking its eye, watching all this unfold with amusement.

"Lock her up," Mrs. Cantanker snapped. "Well, this time, so she can't escape. And then meet me at the mausoleum. Magdeboor returns *tonight.*"

Chapter Twenty-Two

THE dungeon where I was to spend my final hours was little more than a damp, mossy cave. A well covered with a rusting grate stood at its center. A barred window pierced the wall high in one corner. And who should be standing in its cold, pale light but Bram and Minnifer, side by side in their crisp black uniforms. They watched, their faces solemn, as Mr. Grenouille shoved me into the cell. "And stay there!" he said, wagging his finger at me like a stern schoolmaster. Then he locked the gate with a ring of keys and scuttled away.

I kicked the bars once, soundly, with the heel of my

shoe. "Hello," I said, tossing a brief, contemptuous scowl at the servants who were not really servants but who could be practically anyone. "What are you doing here?"

"What are *we* doing here?" Minnifer crept toward me and laid a hand on my arm. "Zita, what happened—?"

I shrugged her off. "You tell me," I said. "Did you run away and betray me as I soon as I was out of sight?"

Minnifer's mouth fell open. Then she hurried back to Bram, casting a suspicious look at me over her shoulder. "D'you think she's possessed? I think so. Probably by a weesht. Probably it caught her as soon as she went up those stairs, and now it's walked her back from the dead like a puppet on a string. Look at that scowl."

"I'm not possessed by anything except maybe a head-ache," I said. "Now tell me who you are and why you're down here."

"They found us," said Bram. "They came trooping along the gallery, bold as brass."

"And so we ran," said Minnifer. "But not fast enough. Those lavender sachets didn't do squat against Gartlut and Mrs. Cantanker. They had us thrown down here. We're prisoners too, don't you see?"

"I don't know *what* you are," I said. "But you're not servants, and you haven't been here for ages like you said. I don't know if anything you've told me was true, or if you were ever really my friends." I bit the inside of my cheek to stop myself from crying. "Just tell me, and please don't lie. Who are you really?"

For a moment there was no sound but water plinking on stone. Then Bram took a deep breath. "We're John and Greta Brydgeborn, apprentices of Georgina Brydgeborn, formerly of Oglethorpe Orphanage, North Hackenden, and since the arrival of Ysabeau Harkleath Cantanker-St. Cloud, servants at Blackbird Castle."

My poor brain, still recovering from being struck by a brick, wobbled inside my skull. "You're *who*?" I managed at last.

But they weren't paying any attention to me. They were staring at each other, and then Minnifer said in a surprised voice, "Nothing happened! Bram, nothing happened!"

"Nothing did," Bram agreed. "D'you suppose it's worn off?"

"Or someone pulled the stitches out—"

Minnifer squealed. Then she gathered a lungful of air and said very quickly, as if expecting her lips to clamp shut at any moment, "Ysabeau Harkleath Cantanker-St. Cloud is an evil villainess who's scheming to end the Brydgeborn line and bring back the Dark Queen Magdeboor."

Bram and Minnifer exchanged glances. Minnifer looked up at the ceiling and clicked her jaw about in an exploratory fashion. And then they were both jabbering at full speed, and it was all I could do to keep up.

"We were hexed," said Minnifer. "We couldn't say our true names, or tell you anything about the fate of the Brydgeborns."

"We couldn't say a word to warn you," said Bram. "About Mrs. Cantanker or Mr. Grenouille or anyone. But we tried. That's why we left clues, and why Greta's book of all things was in the chimney, and why we gave you the skeleton key."

"*You* gave me the skeleton key?" I exclaimed. "No, you didn't! Greta's ghost did. And that's what doesn't make sense. *She* was helping me, but she's also evil and in league with Mrs. Cantanker."

"Greta's ghost?" Minnifer shook her head. "You mean Flora Wheeler? Oh, she most definitely was *not* helping you. She managed to get into the castle during the last hiring, but she was never on our side. You might have thought her and Mrs. Hanguard and that gardener boy were royalty, the way they treated the other servants. And yet there she was, weaving her dark schemes right under all our noses. She didn't give you a thing. She *had* a skeleton key when she was a servant here, and you probably saw her ghost snooping about with it, spying all over the place and threatening the household spirits with nasty punishments if they helped you. But it was us that slipped in and gave you the last of the skeleton keys while you were sleeping. It was *so* cold in there that night, goodness. I still remember. . . ."

"Because she was there," I said. "Greta—I mean

Flora—was in the room, and so was Teenzy, and . . . she was following Teenzy! Teenzy showed me the library, not her."

Minnifer's eyes lit up. "You saw Teenzy?" She sighed. "I haven't seen her in ages, but I thought she might be helping, too. We took care of her after Georgina brought us here, and when Teenzy died, she didn't leave. We always thought she was waiting for you."

Poor Teenzy. Poor all the good ghosts and magical creatures of Blackbird Castle who had watched it fall into disrepair at the hands of these devious people. But it *was* making sense now. Flora Wheeler had simply been another villainess, working with Mrs. Cantanker and Gartlut and all the members of the League of the Blue Spider. She'd infiltrated the castle along with the other false servants, been sacrificed at the dining room table, and then continued her wicked work as a ghost. I'd thought she was on my side, and I'd also thought she was better than I was because she'd looked the part and seemed ever so witchy and glamorous. But she'd been a servant too, and the whole time, a little bit of my real family had been in the kitchens, helping me as best they could.

It's like it doesn't know she's dead, I had told Minnifer the morning after I found her book of all things. Because Greta wasn't dead. Greta—the real Greta—had been next to me the whole time, mending pillowcases and trooping about with buckets.

I ran to Minnifer and hugged her, and then Bram, so tightly it was their turn to go rigid like a pair of hat stands. "I'm sorry," I said, stepping back and grinning ear to ear. "I'm sorry I thought you were wicked. But I'm so happy you're here, and that you've been here all along. I don't know what I would have done without you. Are you witches too?"

Minnifer guffawed. "That depends on who's asking. The villagers would say yes, since we're very odd. And Georgina *did* do her best to prepare us once she realized you might not . . . well, you know. But Bram kept sneaking off to the kitchens to practice his consommés and croquembouches, and once I discovered the secret library it was over for me too. A cozy room full of interesting books is a dangerous thing, let me tell you. Anyway, we never really got the trick of herding ghosts or fighting moorwhistlers, and no birds ever bothered showing up for us either. Once Mrs. Cantanker arrived, we were done for."

"Speaking of which . . . ," Bram said, casting a worried look toward the window. A long, low howl emanated across the gardens, followed by sharp bleating cries and what sounded like animals crashing through Pragast Wood.

"Right," said Minnifer. "Look, Zita, we'll tell you everything we know, but we'd better start finding a way out of here if we're going to survive. You start over there, and Bram, you search there, and I'll see about the well."

We dispersed, investigating every cranny of the dungeon. Minnifer rattled at the well's rusting grate. I scratched around the edge of a loose stone to see if it might reveal a hidden key or a secret door. It revealed only a toothy, many-legged worm that reared up and hissed at me, and I replaced the stone quickly.

We talked while we worked, our whispers bouncing from one corner of the cell to the other. Every few minutes the waistcoated goat creature came clip-clopping down the stairs to peer at us unsettlingly, and our conversation would break off and we would lean against the walls, looking innocently at the ceiling. But as soon as he had gone we would resume, Bram and Minnifer telling me of the evils that had befallen Blackbird Castle.

"It started when you vanished," said Minnifer. "Probably it started long before, but that's when everyone began to see it, like those tiny sprouts that pop up out of the soil from old, old roots. The League of the Blue Spider has been around for a hundred years. It's a whole passel of people wanting Magdeboor to come back from the dead and return the witches to their former glory. But they needed a Brydgeborn for that. And they needed to get past Pragast Wood."

I thought of the nanny in the Black Sitting Room. *A path of salt, a door of ivy. The Butcher of Beydun out in the trees, waiting for me.*

"They did get past Pragast Wood," I said, pulling with all my might at the grate covering the well. It came off in my hands, and I squinted into the seemingly bottomless pit below, wondering at our chances if we tried to climb down it. "They kidnapped me right from under my family's nose. So why didn't they summon Magdeboor back then? I suppose my mother was far too clever to be tricked the way I was, but they might have raised me up to be the perfect little villainess. Why let me go?"

"Your mother made a great sacrifice," said Bram. "The day you were taken, she knew at once what was happening. She went into the underworld and made a bargain with Magdeboor: in ten years' time, she would hand herself over. She would give up her powers and not stand in Magdeboor's way. And in return, Magdeboor and the Butcher were to release you at once."

I remembered suddenly the sparrows in Mrs. Boliver's chimney, how the mother bird sacrificed herself to the flames burning her nest. To the very last, she'd fought, though the fire was too hot and the smoke too thick.

My mother had done the same, traveling into the underworld and promising her own life so that I could live. It hadn't been a wise deal. One daughter was not worth all the evil Magdeboor would spread throughout the world. But somehow, my mother had decided I was.

"And Magdeboor agreed?"

"Of course!" said Minnifer. "What were ten years when she'd been imprisoned for so long? But Magdeboor did not promise to release you anywhere near Blackbird Castle, and your mother had not anticipated such dishonorable deeds. The Butcher let you go, casting a spell so that no one could find you, by magic or otherwise, until the ten years had passed. You lived your life far away from Westval, and Georgina searched and searched for you, hoping to find you and train you in the arts of a Blackbird before it was too late. But she never could."

"And then?" I asked. "What happened then?"

"Then Mrs. Cantanker arrived. It was sure as clockwork, sure as thunder after the lightning. The ten years ended and *she* swept into the castle, an emissary of the

Dark Queen herself. She forced Georgina to give up her powers. And who was left to stand in Magdeboor's way then? Only a lost daughter who didn't know the first thing about witches and was really quite clueless about just about ever— Oh, pardon me."

"It's all right," I said. "I was."

"That's when everything got really bad," said Minnifer. "Georgina managed to convince Mrs. Cantanker not to kill us outright, but this was almost worse. Our hex forbade us from running away, and we couldn't tell anyone anything either. We tried to send a cow down into the valley with a message written on its hide, but not even *that* worked. It all came out gibberish, and who knows if anyone even found the cow. . . ."

"Oh, anyone did," I murmured, thinking of Betsy Gilford and her tales. She hadn't been wrong, and neither had the coachman—strange things *did* happen in Blackbird Castle. But they were stranger than the villagers of Hackenden could ever have dreamed.

I rattled the gate, trying to think of a spell that could

open locks. I knew of several, but they all required star root to startle the metal, and basil cut at perfect forty-five-degree angles to soothe it and make it agreeable. I was not equipped with either.

"So there you have it," said Minnifer. "The Butcher was invited into the lands of the living, where he cast the ephinadym mulsion spell, thus beginning the summoning of Magdeboor. The three servants were dressed up as Brydgeborns and sacrificed in the dining room for her return, and all the other servants ran away, thinking the family was dead. And then Mr. Grenouille wrote that letter and sent the scarecrow off to find you. And oh, did they make a show of it when you arrived! Mrs. Cantanker acted like she loathed you being found."

"I don't think she was acting," I said. "She had to be sure I *was* the missing Brydgeborn. And once she was sure, she had a whole load of other reasons to hate me, what with me being a witch by blood and being allowed all sorts of things no one had ever given her." A thought darted into my mind. "Were they ever really friends?

My mother and Mrs. Cantanker?"

"Best friends," said Minnifer softly. "Long ago. But they chose such different paths."

"Where is my mother?" I asked. "If she's not up in the dining room, did Mrs. Cantanker . . . is she dead?"

"Dead?" Minnifer exclaimed, exchanging a shocked look with Bram. "Well, I told you she was, didn't I . . . all those months ago when you first arrived. But we didn't know then. We didn't know they're keeping her in the mausoleum out beyond the graveyard. We found her on the way back from Amsel's tower the day you went hunting for your Anchor. She's there, Zita, in the little house, and she's quite alive! They brought her this and that to make her comfortable, but it's got to be awful out there—"

"She's alive?" I whispered. I remembered Gartlut and the wheelbarrow, the ghost of Flora Wheeler standing furiously next to that shadowy house in the woods, as if to keep me away. And then I was practically shrieking, hurtling about the room and shouting, *"My mother's alive!"* until quite a few rats and triggles poked their heads out of nooks and cracks to see what all the fuss was about.

"For the moment," said Minnifer, giving me another probing look, as if she still wasn't quite convinced I wasn't possessed. "But she won't be for long. And neither will we, for that matter. We're still stuck."

I pressed my face to the bars, peering down the murky passage. "Well, I don't intend to be stuck much longer," I said. "Remember the skeleton key you gave me?"

Minnifer's face brightened. "You brought it with you?"

"No," I admitted. "The triggles took it after they knocked me over the head. But maybe, just maybe. . . ."

I raced to the window. The sill was well above me, but I stood on tiptoes and stretched my hand out into the cold, damp morning. "Vikers?" I murmured, in as nice a tone as I could muster. "Vikers, my sweet feathery friend? Are you out there?"

At first I felt nothing. Vikers might have flown off, thinking us all a lost cause, and who could blame him? But then my locket pulsed slightly, and I had the sudden impression of wind brushing through feathers, bitter cold, and of gazing down upon the tops of trees.

Vikers! I thought, as the clever little knot of the crow's mind drifted and bumped against my own. I felt him bank sharply, soaring above Westval and the wooded flanks of the mountains. *Vikers, it's possible you don't think much of me anymore now that I've managed to become captured with no chance of escape, and I know I'm probably the most disappointing witch one could be attached to. But better than no witch at all, right? So, here's my trouble: I'm locked in the dungeon of Blackbird Castle with Minnifer and Bram, who are actually Greta and John Brydgeborn. Mrs. Cantanker and Mr. Grenouille and the Butcher of Beydun are setting up some sort of ritual to call back Magdeboor from the dead, and we're going to stop them, but only if we can get out of here. Which is where you come in. The triggles stole my skeleton key. They've probably taken it to Amsel's Tower. Will you go get it and come to the cellars posthaste? Without snapping off any of their heads, please?*

I opened my eyes. Bram and Minnifer were staring at me skeptically.

"Is something supposed to happen?" Minnifer asked.

"Well," I said, "maybe not at once," and I thought, *Please, Vikers. Please come back.*

I paced circles around the well, my hands clasped behind my back. Minnifer and Bram began to argue quietly, throwing concerned looks my way. I wondered if I had imagined Vikers out of sheer desperation.

And then, from far away, I heard a long, piercing *craw!* The craws became louder, the flap of wings too, like a tablecloth being snapped out over and over. The goat-headed creature emerged to investigate, squinting through the bars. But when he heard the distant wing-beats he drew back, clattering away again into the dark. And a moment later, Vikers came careening down the passage, his feathers gleaming green and purple in the dim light. Gripped tightly in his talons was my skeleton key.

"Vikers!" I said, stretching my arm through the bars. "Vikers, it *is* good to see you!"

Vikers did not look opposed to seeing me either. He

dropped the key into my waiting palm and wriggled between the bars, perching on my shoulder and rubbing his head against my cheek.

"Well done," I whispered, scratching Vikers under his beak. And to Bram and Minnifer I said, "I'm going to get my belt and my scissors. And then there's just one more thing I've got to do."

I pushed the key into the lock, its leaf-shaped tines shivering as I twisted it. The gate opened with a creak. And with silver in my pocket, crow feathers tickling my ear, and my friends on either side, I darted down the passageway and up the cellar stairs.

Chapter Twenty-Three

IT could not have been much past ten o'clock in the morning, but as we ran through the freshly fallen snow into the cold embrace of Pragast Wood, it might as well have been midnight. Clouds were spilling across the mountains, closing like a dark lid over the valley. Lightning flashed ominously in the distance, and thunder rumbled, as if even the weather could tell something unholy was on its way and was rushing in to watch.

We were not alone under the trees. Ghosts drifted in the eddies of snow and fog, strange, misshapen creatures, their toes floating inches above the ground. They paid no attention to us. We darted from tree to tree, Bram and Minnifer in green cloaks, me in the dark uniform of a Blackbird. We did not blend in at all, but the ghosts never even turned their heads to look at us. They were all moving in the same direction, like boats in a current, straight for the graveyard and Magdeboor's mausoleum.

"D'you see that?" Minnifer whispered, as we gathered behind a gnarled oak to catch our breath. "D'you see that light?"

A bloody glow was blooming against the black branches beyond the graveyard. It was as if a flaming maw had opened in the darkest depths of Pragast Wood, and now all the spirits and evil things that had piled up against the protective wards and sigils of the castle were being drawn to it. I swallowed. Somewhere at the heart of that crimson smudge was Magdeboor's little stone mansion, and inside it was my mother. . . .

We began to run again. In the sky above, Vikers gave a warning cry, but we were not about to turn back now.

My locket was in my hand. My silver scissors dangled from my belt, and I clutched a sharply pointed candlestick to my chest. I'd taken it from the castle for good measure, in case my spells and herbs failed me. Bram and Minnifer were similarly armed, Bram with a fire poker and Minnifer with an enormous cudgel that she'd dragged out of the pantry.

We skirted the graveyard and arrived at the mausoleum, creeping up through the underbrush that grew against its side. The red glow was coming from inside the tomb, bleeding from the doorway and from what must have been a window at its back. It was a strange, unsteady light, flickering ruddily and sending twisting shadows toward the sky.

The mausoleum's iron doors—carved with ravens and pockmarked with moss—hung open. Voices echoed out, an entire convention of them. I recognized Mrs. Cantanker's hiss, Gartlut's and Mr. Grenouille's mutters. And then a fourth voice, softer, but stern and commanding.

Mother?

"Shut up," I heard Mrs. Cantanker snap. "You too, Charles. Pigtooth? Pigtooth, go to the cellars. Bring Zita here. I see no reason to keep Magdeboor waiting until nightfall simply for aesthetics."

We pressed ourselves to the side of the mausoleum. Hooves clattered over stone as something made its way down the steps and into the woods.

"To the back," I murmured to Bram and Minnifer. "To the window. I'm going to take a look."

I was grateful for the powdery snow as we shuffled around the back of the mausoleum. Old snow would have crunched and cracked and given us away, but in this our feet sank with hardly a sound. The mausoleum's only window was shaped like a wedge of fruit. Red light oozed from it, staining the whiteness. I saw the spirits and the beasts, still approaching through the trees, drawn to the glow like moths. They formed a ring around the mausoleum, swaying, their eyes empty and blank.

"Bram," I whispered, planting my candlestick point

down in the snow. "Will you let me stand on your shoulders?"

Bram nodded. Minnifer laced her fingers together, launching me up onto Bram's shoulder. I pressed my face to the window.

A strange scene greeted me. The mausoleum's interior had been furnished quite comfortably for my mother's use. It was still a grim place, moss and black stone, the corners piled with dead leaves that had blown in through the doors. But beeswax candles dripped everywhere, and there were several tasseled rugs, and even piles of silk cushions and a little painted dresser with a set of porcelain tea things on a tray. Mrs. Cantanker was there, pacing to and fro in her red gown. Gartlut was back to looking like a regular oaf, the Butcher having no doubt crawled back inside his body, and Mr. Grenouille, and several ladies and gentlemen I recognized from the ballroom stood in one corner, heads together. The place would have looked like a cozy garden cottage were it not for the great stone coffin at its center. The coffin was open, and the red light that stained the woods and colored my cheeks was coming from *inside* it, pouring out like flames.

I gasped, wobbling on Bram's shoulders. Something was in that coffin—a dark shape, lying still. I turned my face away, searching for my mother. She was sitting in a gilt chair, looking tired and weak. But she was alive, and the sight of her made my heart sing. She was not just a tiny moving picture in a locket anymore, or a fleeting scent of violets and rosemary, and she didn't look like Mrs. Hanguard the housekeeper at all. Memories flooded over me.

I saw her at breakfast, looking out the window at the woods. I saw her leading me to the Tiny Queen's Throne Room and allowing me to peek inside its little door. I saw us at Christmas, climbing the great spruce, and her lifting me up so I could place a silver moon at its top. I saw her the morning I vanished, me sitting in her lap and her reading to me from a little book of tales. Then she'd been called away—she was very busy, after all, and very important—and I'd watched her go, her white dress flickering down the dark corridor. The nanny had come then, leading me outside and pointing me toward the woods. And there stood the Butcher, calling to me, his voice like winter—

I snapped back to the present. The ladies and gentlemen from the League of the Blue Spider were milling around my mother, and she sat in her chair, straight-backed and regal, confusing them all with her fearlessness.

"Do not assume you've won, Ysabeau," I heard her say. "My daughter is a clever girl, and if she is still in the lands of the living, fate might yet take a very different turn."

"Oh, be quiet, Georgina," Mrs. Cantanker snapped. "Don't make me regret sparing your life. The fate of everyone is *quite* decided, thank you very much. And yours is too. I gave you your chance. I tried to make you see. But you remain stubborn. I can't imagine Magdeboor will be at all pleased to see you when she gets here."

I cast a frightened glance down at Bram and Minnifer. "We've got to get inside," I whispered. "I think they're going to do so something to Mother."

I turned back to the window . . . and there, its face pressed to the glass, its puffy hands on either side, was a triggle. My eyes widened. The triggle's eyes did too. We gaped at each other for a long moment, unblinking. Then the triggle threw back its head and let out a piercing, deafening wail.

Bram wobbled.

Minnifer began to hiss frantically, things like, "What's that? Shut it up, Zita, shut it up!"

And in the mausoleum, seven faces turned to peer up at the window. Mrs. Cantanker's expression twisted into one of utter hatred. I tipped backward, losing my balance. And then Bram fell, too, and we both landed with a *whump* in the snow.

The beasts were upon us in seconds. I had not even shaken the stars from my head when Mr. Grenouille and a host of moorwhistlers and misshapen ghosts had me by the arms and were dragging me to my feet.

"Minnifer!" I shouted. "Bram!" But I couldn't see them, and Vikers felt a thousand miles away. I heard a crashing and a faint *Oof!* Then I was being herded up the steps and through the doors. The creatures clustered around me, faces pressing in. My scissors and belt were taken from me and thrown into a corner.

"Zita?" Mother looked up from her chair. She tried to rise, but the chair's arms sprouted wooden hands that gripped her and pulled her back. "Zita, oh, heavens, is it you?"

I spun, squinting through the shadows and the flickering light. I tried to run to her, but Gartlut, Mr. Grenouille, and Mrs. Cantanker surrounded me. For a brief moment, I heard Bram and Minnifer yelling outside. Then the iron doors slammed shut, cutting off the sounds from the woods.

"Well, well," said Mrs. Cantanker, grinning down at me. "As always, my dear, you are rather *too* punctual." She turned to Gartlut. "Do it now."

Mother struggled again to rise, her eyes wide and frightened. I saw her mouth something—a spell perhaps—but nothing happened. She had given up her powers, bargained them away to save my life.

"The blood of the Brydgeborns bound Magdeboor and cast her out of the lands of the living," intoned Mrs. Cantanker, her voice echoing. "And only the blood of the Brydgeborns can bring her back." She drew a knife from inside her sleeve, a pale, curved slash of bone, sharpened to a point, its blade so thin it could pare a stalk of grass down to threads, cut skin like silk. . . .

I screamed, lashing out against Gartlut and Mr. Grenouille. I tried to think of something to help me, anything. My mind was blank with terror. They were dragging me toward that open coffin, and a horrid stench of rot and decay was oozing into my nose, followed by a wave of brimstone, fire, and smoke.

I did not want to see inside the coffin. I didn't think I could bear it. But they dragged me to its edge. I felt the heat boiling out of it, beating against my face. And there she was: the ancient witch, the Dark Queen, Magdeboor Brydgeborn.

She was floating, hovering above a seemingly bottomless pit of fire. Her skin was white, unblemished by rot. Her raven tresses spread about her like a writhing halo. She wore her battle gear, a suit of armor, gauntlets with nails like thorns, and in one skeletal hand, clutched tightly, was a gold coin.

"Zita!" I heard my mother's scream from far away. "Don't let them wake her! Don't let them!"

I didn't want to let them. But they pinned my wrist against the stone, my hand just over Magdeboor's face. The tip of the knife bit into my finger. . . .

The droplet of blood fell slowly, like a beautiful glinting ruby. It touched Magdeboor's forehead, beading there for a moment. Then it sank into her papery skin, like water into thirsty soil, and she blinked.

Chapter Twenty-Four

MAGDEBOOR stood, floating upright above the fiery pit, her arms hanging limp at her sides. Then she stepped solidly onto the stone edge of the coffin, her armored feet clanking. She was not very tall. In fact, she was barely as tall as I was. But there was something huge about her, a power that flowed from her and made everyone around her seem delicate and brittle. The ghosts shuddered and drew back. Outside, a howl went up, whether in celebration or terror, I didn't know. She still looked like the girl in the painting. But that girl had been young and innocent. This was a dead thing, hollowed out of all that had once been good. This was one who had seen hell.

"Our queen," Mrs. Cantanker breathed, sweeping into a low bow. "Welcome back."

Magdeboor surveyed Mrs. Cantanker briefly, her gaze black and glinting. Mrs. Cantanker, still bowing, rolled her eyes upward, perhaps to see what effect her display was having. Then she shivered slightly, and I had never seen her look so afraid.

"My lady," said Mrs. Cantanker, rising. "Your house awaits, cleansed of the Brydgeborns who threw you out. And an army too, ten thousand souls eager to follow you into battle." She gestured toward the gathered villains. "We are your humble servants. All but *her.*"

She pointed, and Magdeboor's eyes slid slowly to me. She looked me up and down. Then she swept forward, her wild hair floating around her, her face placid. An icy wind accompanied her, sending leaves fleeing like a million tiny burning soldiers before a dragon.

"You are not my humble servant?" she asked, in a deep, commanding voice. "You are not on my side?"

I didn't reply. Instead I kicked viciously at Mr. Grenouille, striking him in the leg. He let out a yelp and lost hold of me, and I stumbled away, staring about at the hideous tableau of witches and monsters.

"And yet you seem so like me." Magdeboor was in front of me suddenly, trailing a hand along my cheek. She stank terribly, and she had moved like a breath, like a phantom. Once again I felt her power, hateful and huge, coursing through her veins and pulsing beneath her skin.

"Are you going to kill me?" I asked.

She laughed. At her side, Gartlut laughed too, and then he began to sag, the Butcher of Beydun climbing out of him, long white arms extending like spiders' legs from Gartlut's mouth.

"Perhaps," she said. "Perhaps not. I do not kill witches unless they turn against me. Have you turned against me? Have not your works summoned me, and your blood brought me here?"

"*I* brought you here," said Mrs. Cantanker, scooting

in front of me. "My queen, I did this. I brought back the Butcher too, your truest friend. All is ready—"

"Quiet!" Magdeboor roared, and Mrs. Cantanker flinched as if she'd been slapped. Magdeboor turned slowly to look at her. "And who are you? Not a witch, I see."

"No," said Mrs. Cantanker, in a tiny, tiny voice. "But . . . *I* did this. I did this for you!"

"And yet you are not one of us," said Magdeboor. "You have powdered your face and painted your hair with raven dye . . . but you are not one of us. You are that breed of creature that sticks like fleas to a dog's tail, like lice to an urchin's head. You cannot fathom power. You can only gather the scraps."

Mrs. Cantanker was shaking. "The darkness takes everyone," she'd said. "The darkness wasn't too good to have me." But the darkness cared nothing for you once it had gotten all it could take. I wondered if she would see how foolish she'd been, if she'd abandon her horrid plans and help me instead. . . .

"I *am* your faithful servant," she whispered. "To the end."

Magdeboor nodded slightly. Then she turned away, dismissing Mrs. Cantanker as if she were no more than a fly. Magdeboor began circling me slowly, her dead eyes skittering over me. "Georgina Brydgeborn's daughter," she murmured. "The very last of our line. Your mother I do not care for. But you . . . You're not much like her, are you?"

"Don't listen to her, Zita—" Mother started to say.

Magdeboor snapped her fingers. All sound ceased, a shroud of fog enveloping us until there was nothing but me and her, facing each other.

"I feel a fire in you," she said, plucking at my hair. "Pride. Strength. *Ambition.* Some dark clay that might yet be molded. You see a road stretching ahead of you. You've no idea where it leads, but you know—somehow you just *know*—that you are destined for greater things. You've always felt it, haven't you?"

Had I? Months ago, I'd pressed my nose to the post coach's window and wished only for a creaking garden gate and warm embraces. But I hadn't known anything of the world then, hadn't even dreamed of what I might have the power to do.

"Zita?" My mother's voice tore through whatever veil Magdeboor had constructed, stinging my ears. "Zita, don't listen to her! She's a bitter, twisted creature! She's killed and maimed and hurt—"

Magdeboor swept out one hand. The fog dispersed. Everyone in the room went hurtling backward and were pinned to the walls, their mouths shut tight. I was thrown back too, collapsing in a heap against the sarcophagus.

"They don't understand," Magdeboor said, leaning over me. "They're not *real* witches. They let themselves be locked in golden cages, pretty birds with clipped wings. And for what? To please the weak, worthless creatures of this world. Do you think that right, child? Do you think that *fair*?"

"I don't know," I whispered, as Magdeboor whirled around me, the burning cold flowing off her, her glittering gaze fixing me like a needle through an insect.

"Come now," Magdeboor said, lifting me to my feet.

"Of course it isn't fair. We have the gifts to do more. To pass beyond the silly contrivances of life and to taste the wild freedoms beyond the veil. It opens one's mind, you know, traveling there. It makes one see how stupid everyone really is. In the lands of the living, they want only to keep us small—the villagers in Hackenden, the kings of Westval, even my sisters. They want us to play by the rules so that everyone can get along. But they never tell you why you ought to *care* whether everyone gets along. If you're a weak little thing, of course you must. You must cower and beg, and hope for the best. But I am not a weak little thing. Are you?"

"No," I said uncertainly. What was she trying to say?

"Good," she said. "And that is why I will give you a choice. Renounce this world, its pumping veins and heaving lungs. Embrace power." She drew something up out of thin air: a book and a quill. "It's not so very hard to do. I did it once, ages ago. Just give him a little drop of blood, sign a little book. . . ."

"Him?" I whispered. "Is that the Butcher's book?"

"A noble creature, yes," said Magdeboor. "A scion of the underworld, and ever so kind to his subjects."

I almost snorted. How stupid did she think I was? I'd seen what kindnesses she'd shown Mrs. Cantanker, and what kindnesses the Butcher had shown me. And yet she only half smiled again, seeming to read the disbelief from my face.

"You think me mad. And yet if you join our ranks you will never be unsure again, never weak or cold like a mortal witch. You will give your life to the Butcher, as I once did, and you will become a dark princess. The power he grants is nothing to scoff at, and both the lands of the living and of the dead will cower at our feet."

"I'll die," I said.

"In a way. But one spares oneself all sorts of troubles by dying."

"And if I don't?"

"If you don't? Then you will live! But you will live as a sniveling housemaid, and you'll always remember how you could have been so much more, but you chose not to."

My head was spinning. I wasn't going to sign anything Magdeboor gave me. And yet one little part of me had been listening to her.

"What about Mother? If I sign it, will you let her live?"

Magdeboor looked at me sharply for a moment. Then her head twitched such a little bit, as if a thought had just flown into it, and she said, "Of course! You may do with her as you please. Think of it this way: You could be like your mother, if you signed this book. She too made a great sacrifice. A great sacrifice for a great reward. In the end, you could finally be like her."

Me? Like my mother?

I took the quill from Magdeboor's hand. Its tip glimmered, sharp and cruel, and Magdeboor enfolded me in her black cloak, the mist, the cold, and the fire swirling around me. My hand hovered just above the book, the quill pinched tightly.

"Sign it, Zita," she hissed in my ear. "What has life given you that you owe it anything at all?"

My locket was burning against my skin, uncomfortably

hot. What *had* life given me? I'd been cold and hungry for most of it. I'd worked my fingers raw, been screamed at by Mrs. Boliver, and then gone to seek my fortune in a haunted castle and nearly been killed on multiple occasions. I wondered what Magdeboor might teach me, what a magnificent creature I might become. Would I be rich and beautiful like Mrs. Cantanker, as powerful as the Dark Queen as herself?

But then, from inside the locket, I heard a voice, gentle and sweet . . . my mother singing a lullaby. And suddenly the grand illusions vanished. I thought of my friends at the orphanage handing me the wooden comb they'd bought. I thought of Bram and Minnifer by the fire, Vikers, and Teenzy, even the kind old woman on the coach who had shared her plums with me. I thought of my mother going to the very bottom of the underworld to rescue me, my father searching for me until the day he died. . . . They had not done it for a great reward. They had done it because it was right and good. And perhaps they had been *too* good, too trusting, for they had failed.

My mother had fallen for Magdeboor's tricks, her promises, and her lies. But I had learned my lesson there.

"Some things just are." That was true. But in a witch's house, nothing is as it seems. There was the outside of things and the inside, and I no longer believed in the outsides of things.

I whirled and plunged the pointy end of the quill into Magdeboor's arm, right at the joint in her armor. Then I wrenched away from her and ran, pelting across the tomb toward my scissors.

Magdeboor screamed. I grasped the scissors seconds before I was sent flying backward, through the doors and into the icy darkness of the woods.

"I gave you a chance!" Magdeboor bellowed, striding out of the mausoleum. "I gave you a chance to be strong! You think you can be kind and still be powerful? Well, you cannot."

That's what she said, but I didn't have to believe her. I stood shakily, brushing the snow from my cloak. Then I squared my shoulders, facing Magdeboor as she reared up in front of me. The bone knife was in her hand, its point still stained with my blood, but I did not flinch.

"You had me kidnapped," I said slowly, the words dropping like bitter herbs from my mouth. "You hurt my family and tricked my parents. I don't know if I'm like my mother. But I'll *never* be like you."

I lifted my hand. In it, my locket glowed bright as a silver star, pushing the red flames away and blowing the snow back in a great arc.

"An Anchor?" Magdeboor laughed. "Oh, I'm terrified. What do you propose to do with that? You're hardly old enough to be much of a Blackbird, and you're all alone—"

"That's where you're wrong," I said, raising the locket higher still. And then from far away came a sound. It began as a rumbling, a thunder in the ground. The snow trembled slightly. The woods creaked. Next came a roar, deep and bellowing, and the snap of branches. And then, slithering and pounding through the trees toward us, was a dragon. It still looked like a staircase, black wood and gilt, treads running up its back, and a banister too. But the red glow in its veins was brighter now. Its wooden wings were extended, its jeweled eyes open wide, rosettes of ruby and emerald. Running beside it was Teenzy, and following her were a hundred household spirits, the Bellamy ghost, even the seventeen bull-dogs from the Library of Souls, and a certain Telurian prince in a tricorn hat, now free of his marble bust and looking very dashing indeed. In the sky above, Vikers let out a triumphant screech.

Magdeboor's eyes widened. I felt a glow in my heart, like fire, like sunlight on autumn leaves. It hadn't taken me long to wake the staircase. I still had the treskgilliam twig, my Anchor, and my scissors. Rose petals and blackberry branches had been quickly procured, and Bram and Minnifer had helped me clip the thorns and lay them around the staircase. At first it had not responded. It had released a puff of smoke from its nostrils and curled up, as if to sleep some more. But I had given it a firm tap on its snout and said, "In twenty minutes you'll be on your feet, please, and headed for Magdeboor's mausoleum in the woods, is that clear? And not a moment longer, or you'll have a new mistress, and she won't be half as nice as me."

Now the dragon pushed between the trees and into the clearing, releasing another roar that set the moorwhistlers and weeshts to shivering. From somewhere close by, I heard Bram and Minnifer let out a cheer, and then I saw Minnifer dodging the grip of a specter, picking up her cudgel and swinging it wildly around her.

"Get my mother!" I shouted to her. "Get her out of the mausoleum, chair and all if you have to!" Then I dashed up the stairs along the dragon's back and situated myself behind its horns. Vikers landed on my shoulder, Teenzy climbed into my lap, cold and soft as a winter cloud. I whispered a kindly word into the dragon's ear, and it reared up over Magdeboor, its wings blotting out the sky.

"I'm Zita Brydgeborn!" I shouted down. "Last of my name. And you're *all* trespassing."

The dragon pounced. Its tail slashed through the air,

splintering trees. Magdeboor dove out of the way, her beasts scattering, flying into the woods and vanishing into tombs and the hollows of trees.

But Magdeboor did not flee. She skittered up a tree, quick as a spider, the bone knife clutched to her chest, and there she began to speak quietly, her eyes pooling with red light. A high, whistling note rang through the woods—a call like the one I used to summon Vikers. Again the woods seemed to tremble and groan, the trees crackling with the approach of a massive shape.

I had not expected to see another fangore in my life, certainly not one larger and more hideous than the one I'd conquered. But here one was, loping from among the trees, ten times the size of the last one, its belly fat with spirits, their faces squashed, bulbous-eyed, against its ropy vines and sinew. Magdeboor leaped from her tree and climbed onto its back, scaling its neck in seconds. And we faced each other in the clearing—a dragon, a dead thing, and two very different witches, one wrapped in shadows, the other wreathed in silver light.

Magdeboor bared her teeth. "You might have lived," she said. "Or you might have died a queen, and become a powerful, wondrous creature of the dark. But now you will die a housemaid, and there'll be no mercy from me, no gifts or promises for your journeys ahead."

"I don't want your gifts!" I shouted, but it was lost in the dragon's roar. The fangore wailed in response, high and harrowing. And then I was hanging on for dear life as they charged each other across the clearing. I caught a glimpse of Minnifer and Bram fighting their way into the mausoleum. Then the two monsters collided, and I was nearly thrown from my perch.

A clawed arm caught the dragon in the neck, heaving it to the side and leaving deep gouges in its polished black wood. Vikers and Teenzy leaped onto the fangore, attacking Magdeboor in a screeching frenzy of fur and feathers. My dragon regained its balance, its jaws opening wide. Something rumbled and boiled up the length of it, and then it blew a blast of red flame at the fangore, enveloping Magdeboor and turning the snow to rippling steam.

But Magdeboor seemed to relish the heat, extending her arms as if sinking into a warm bath. The fangore swung at the dragon again, burning now. Wood cracked. Then Magdeboor leaped from her mount onto mine, her bone knife nearly taking off my head.

I ducked, felt it singing over me. When she struck again, I gripped my silver scissors and caught her blade with my own, twisting it away.

"So you're not alone," she spat, leering down at me. "But you're still weak. Household ghosts, wandering souls too frightened to face the underworld, a handful of servants, and a witch who sacrificed her powers for nothing? Who would even *want* friends like that?"

I would, I thought, gritting my teeth as she struck at me again and again. Then I rolled away from her, bouncing and falling down the stairs. Magdeboor flew after me like some vengeful bird of prey, dodging the claws and wings of our battling beasts. The fangore's tail scythed through the air. I squirmed around onto my back just in time to see Magdeboor bending over me.

She gripped me around the neck, lifting me right off my feet. Her gauntlet bit into my skin. My eyes bulged, and I gasped, clutching at her wrist.

The dragon let out a horrible groan, as if it could feel my pain. It lowered itself to the ground, writhing, and the fangore loomed over us all, the souls in its belly howling wildly.

Magdeboor began to drone on and on about Westval, and the spirit realm, and all the folk who had wronged her. But I had no time for her grudges. I looked past her, her face blurring, and caught the eye of one of the ghosts peering from the leaves of the fangore's stomach. I managed a wink. It was a friendly wink, a wink that said, "I mean you no harm. I won't attack you with scissors like I did the fangore in the training hall, or force you into formations like the toads on the castle lawn, or jumble you up and herd you along like the clouds in the sky. But if you help me, perhaps one day down the road, I will be able to help you too."

The ghost looked surprised at my wink. And then it winked back.

"Why are you winking, mad child?" Magdeboor

snapped, her fingers tightening around my neck. "Has the last of the Brydgeborns gone mad?"

But even as she spoke, the ghost I had winked at began to wriggle and move among the other ghosts. Pointy elbows poked eyes, and pale feet stepped on faces, and then the fangore's entire stomach began to roil, as if it had eaten something horrible.

Magdeboor spun. "Stop that!" she shouted up at the beast. "Pull yourself together. Finish the dragon, and I will finish the girl—"

But the fangore was not listening. It stood on its hind legs, clutching its stomach. The souls in its belly now seemed to be in full rebellion. Magdeboor stared at me in confusion. And then I knocked her squarely between the eyes.

My shin struck the stair when I dropped, but I was up in an instant, shoving Magdeboor over the banister and running unsteadily for the dragon's head. I reached it and stood between its horns, looking down. The wind blew open my cloak, baring the locket, which glowed bright and silver as starlight.

In the clearing below, Magdeboor pushed herself to her feet. "What have you done?" she demanded. "What have you done to my fangore?"

Souls were crawling from its mouth, dribbling down its chin. They skittered toward Magdeboor, tightening around her like a noose. Mrs. Cantanker emerged onto the steps of the mausoleum, staring in horror at the chaos in the clearing. The Butcher was careening toward Magdeboor, his long white arms outstretched. And there were Bram and Minnifer dragging Mother, chair and all, through the snow, the three of them watching me with looks of joy on their faces.

Cinders and sparrows, I thought, and I felt the dragon beneath me, the ancient trees above me, and the wind in the sky. *Or fire and crows? A witch? A housemaid? A Brydgeborn or an orphan?* In that moment, none of it mattered. They were all words, lids for pots in a pantry. "Some things just *are,*" Mother had said, and in that moment, I simply was.

The locket flashed. The wind howled, and Magdeboor

screamed, the spirits closing over her, bony limbs carrying her back into the mausoleum and the buzzing red light. The Butcher, caught up in their flow, began to writhe and screech, his arms reaching helplessly toward the sky. And then Mrs. Cantanker and the other ladies and gentlemen were overrun too, and sped into the mausoleum, and the iron doors slammed shut.

Magdeboor died for the second time the way I supposed people like her ought to die: dragged into the pits of hell by a swarm of ghosts and taking all her compatriots with her.

When the last cry from the mausoleum had faded, the curse on Mother's chair withered, and she stood. I ran to her and she held me tightly, while a crow, two former orphans, and a higgledy-piggledy army of household ghosts stood quietly by and watched.

"Welcome back, my dear," Mother said, smiling down at me, and all together we went up the dragon staircase, Bram, Minnifer, Teenzy, Vikers, Mother, and me. I took hold of the dragon's horns. For a moment I thought I saw the faintest flicker of red from under the doors of the mausoleum, a finger of light reaching out and then extinguishing as the ghosts closed the sarcophagus and shut our enemies away.

Good riddance, I thought, turning the dragon toward Blackbird Castle. *And good luck.* They would need it on the journey ahead.

Epilogue

"DO you have a larger pair of shears?" I asked, emerging from under a banbristle shrub and squinting up at Mr. Paldome. He was the new gardener and he was standing against the sun, gaping down at me as if I were a poisonous snake that had just popped out of a bathroom drain.

"Well, miss . . . ," he said. "I do somewhere, it's just . . . well, I don't know if—"

"You don't know if you want to hand them over to a witch," I said, and smiled at him. "Well, Mr. Paldome, I'll tell you something . . . and you can tell Betsy Gilford this too, and anyone else who likes to spread tales." I stood and leaned toward him, as if to whisper some great secret. "We don't actually do anything very interesting up here. It's mostly herbology, cutting lavender at a forty-five-degree angle, that sort of thing. And I've never eaten a heart in my life."

He didn't seem to believe me, but he got me the shears and I set back to work on the banbristle until I had an entire bag of bitter-smelling nubs, which I was going to use for my lessons the next day. Mother had told me banbristle nubs banished triggles much more effectively than lavender.

"Thank you," I said when I'd finished, and handed Mr. Paldome back his shears. He tipped his hat, rather nervously, and I tipped mine, and then I headed quickly across the lawn toward the castle. Teenzy materialized next to me, a little burst of coal smoke trotting along by my ankles and looking up at me. I was glad she'd waited for me, and I hoped she'd never go away.

Vikers landed on my shoulder. He kept careful watch over the attention I showed Teenzy, and when he felt it was too much (and he *always* felt it was too much), he became grouchy and looked at me sideways. Sometimes Teenzy leaped about and barked at Vikers, trying to get him to play, at which point Vikers would hunch into his feathers in despair. Now he looked at me imploringly, as if to say, "Why don't you just banish it? It's obnoxious, and it snores, and ghosts don't even have to snore if they don't want to. It's doing it on purpose." But I suspected they'd get used to each other eventually. "I like you both the same," I said, rubbing Vikers under his beak while Teenzy nuzzled my hand. One was warm, the other cold as winter.

It was a bright day, one month after the second fall of Magdeboor. The snow had all but melted. The air was soft and balmy, and the fog was burning away, turning to mist in the watery light. The woods loomed, not forbidding anymore, but rather old and sleepy, protective of the strange world they harbored. Vikers flew off to hunt mice, and Teenzy vanished in a puff of smoke, and I spotted Bram and Minnifer—or Greta and John, though

I don't think I would ever quite get used to calling them that—sitting on a bench, laughing at me.

"You could have helped instead of giggling," I called to them, wiping my hands on my apron. "Or are you both too grand now?"

Minnifer was dressed in a blue coat and great fluffy hat, her face rosy. Bram had on a proper suit and shirt cuffs. He looked merry again, as if his little rain cloud had floated away.

"Never too grand to frighten the gardeners," said Minnifer. "It's just that Mr. Paldome is going to go home this evening, and everyone's going to ask about his day at Blackbird Castle, and you *know* he's going to make something up about being chased by a witch with a pair of shears."

I laughed and shook my head, and together we headed up the slope toward the castle. Through the open windows I could hear workmen banging about, occasionally bellowing rudely when something not entirely alive accosted them. I heard the opening and closing of doors,

Mother calling to one of the maids about where to set a pile of manuscripts, the dragon staircase shifting and creaking in its old place in the great hall.

"It'll be odd having a house full of living things again," said John. "We'll have to get used to that."

"I'm used to it already," said Greta. "Though I bet we'll forget sometimes we're not Bram and Minnifer anymore, and accidentally wake up in the kitchens. Do you bet, John? A chocolate dollar?"

"No," said John. "You'd win. I'll be in the kitchens every day, I think, and I don't intend to do anything heroic ever again."

We stepped through the glass doors of the morning room. The house was being aired and scrubbed. An army of servants trooped through it, buckets steaming, the air sharp with the tang of vinegar and polish. Triggles still bobbed along the shelves, stealing the golden teaspoons and chittering to each other, but the last of the ghouls and moorwhistlers had been sent back to the underworld, and the shadows had dispersed. On the table, spread between the breakfast china and the silverware, were notes and documents organizing the year ahead, spring and summer and then another autumn and another winter. It all stretched ahead of me—a long road, but I was glad to be traveling it.

"One spares oneself all sorts of troubles by dying," Mrs. Cantanker had said once, and Magdeboor had said it too, and they were each just as wrong as the other. One simply lost all the chances one might have had, and skipped all the paths one might have taken.

I'd take the troubles. I'd gather them in my arms and pile them onto my back until I was doubled over like a tinker, and in the meantime I'd see the sun in the puddles, and the flowers growing along the ditch. When I lifted my eyes, I'd see the kind faces among the pale, angry ones, and if I ever met a girl on a post coach I would share my plums with her. When it was all over, and I was an old lady, like Mrs. Boliver, that great big heap on my back would turn into a light as bright as a dozen lanterns, and I'd carry it across the marshes into whatever lay beyond. I was not afraid of life.

John and Greta busied themselves in the morning room, filling their plates with breakfast, but I walked on into the great hall just to stand for a moment by myself. The hall had seemed so grand all those months ago when I'd first arrived with my new hat and my carpetbag. It hadn't changed. The lamps were lit and the floor had been swept and polished, but it was just as impressive as it always had been. Only I did not feel lost in it anymore. I felt it at my fingertips, under my shoes, as if roots were snaking out of me, stitching me up with it. I was a Brydgeborn of Blackbird Castle, and I had come home.